	DATE DUE		

by CONRAD RICHTER

THESE ARE BORZOI BOOKS, PUBLISHED IN NEW YORK BY
Alfred A. Knopf

A COUNTRY

OF STRANGERS

_____

A
COUNTRY
OF
STRANGERS

CONRAD RICHTER

NEW YORK: ALFRED·A·KNOPF: 1971

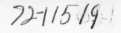

THIS IS A BORZOI BOOK
PUBLISHED BY ALFRED A. KNOPF, INC.

Published May 16, 1966
Reprinted Four Times
Sixth Printing, March, 1971

© Copyright 1966 by Conrad Richter
All rights reserved under International and Pan-American
Copyright Conventions. Distributed by Random House, Inc.
Published simultaneously in Toronto, Canada, by Random
House of Canada Limited.

Library of Congress Catalog Card Number: 66-14921

Manufactured in the United States of America

For Alfred

Oft it befalls   by the grace of God
That into this world   woman and man
Bring child to birth.   They dress it in colors,
Love it and train it   till time shall come
When its limbs are sturdy   and strong with life.
Father and mother   carry and lead it,
Feed it and clothe it   but God alone knows
What the years may give   for the growing child!

Fates of Men,
Exeter Book, Old English,
8th or 9th Century

Charles W. Kennedy's translation into alliterative
verse of *Fates of Men* from the Exeter Book is from
An Anthology of Old English Poetry, © 1960 by
Oxford University Press, Inc.

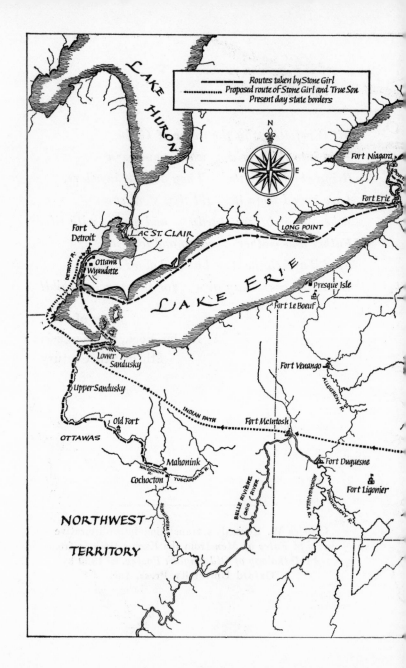

Routes taken by Stone Girl
Proposed route of Stone Girl and True Son
Present day state borders

LAKE HURON

Fort Niagara

Fort Erie

Fort Detroit

LAC ST. CLAIR

Ottawa
Wyandotte

LONG POINT

LAKE ERIE

Presque Isle

Fort Le Boeuf

Lower Sandusky

Fort Venango

Upper Sandusky

INDIAN PATH

Fort McIntosh

Old Fort

OTTAWAS

Mahonink

Cochocton

TUSCARAWAS R.

Fort Duquesne

BELLE RIVIÈRE

OHIO RIVER

Fort Ligonier

NORTHWEST

TERRITORY

MUSKINGUM R.

WALHONDING R.

DETROIT R.

ALLEGHENY R.

MONONGAHELA R.

YOUGHIOGHENY R.

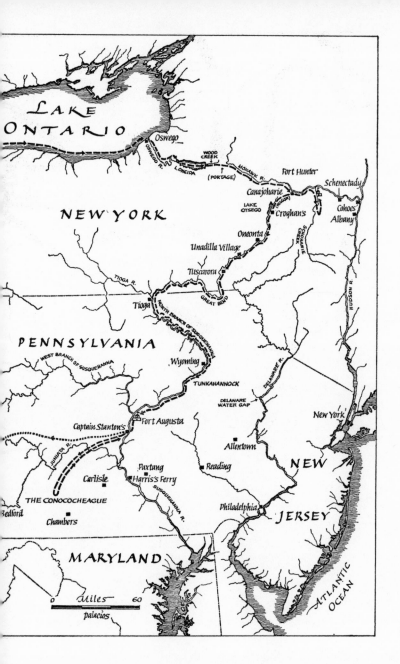

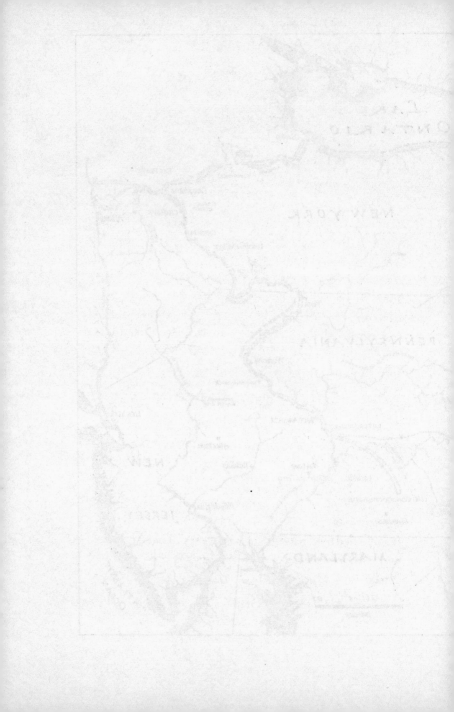

Foreword

LIKE its earlier companion novel, *The Light in the Forest*, this tale concerns the fortunes of one of many white captives taken prisoner as children and adopted into families of the early Indians. When later forcibly returned to their white homes, no small number of these tried desperately to run away and return to the free wild life of the forest and to their Indian fathers and mothers whom they admired and considered their real parents.

In *The Trees* and *The Town* I have written of the Indian from the white man's point of view. Here I would like to continue the design of *The Light in the Forest*, which observes the white man from the viewpoint of that not ignoble race which once called this continent home but whose people were deprived, often rooked, of their rights and lands; their native conceptions of primitive justice and national defense cried out against; their very presence hated and despised; their reduced numbers, never large in the first place, driven from exile to exile; their

solemn treaties with us repeatedly broken by their
"white fathers"; their poetic, generally honorable
and childlike savage nature corrupted by the white
man's perfidy, liquor, and disease until their fate
today remains a blot on our national conscience.

I gratefully acknowledge my debt to the following: Heckwelder's *Memoirs of the Indian Nations*;
Brinton and Anthony's *Lenape-English Dictionary*;
The First Michigan Frontier by Goodrich; the Zeis-
berger writings; *The American Indian* by Haines;
Donehoo's *Indian Villages of Pennsylvania*; Hunter's *Forts on the Pennsylvania Frontier*; Kennedy's
Anthology of Old English Poetry; the historical
accounts of Wing and Rupp; and to other volumes
suggested or made available by Donald H. Kent of
the Pennsylvania Historical Commission, who also
furnished rare old maps; Charles W. Ness of the
Pennsylvania State Library; Genevieve Porter of
the Library of the University of New Mexico;
Robert H. Land of the Library of Congress; D. W.
Thompson of Carlisle, a collector of early Pennsyl-
vaniana; Martha W. McCann of the Detroit Histor-
ical Museum; the Burton Collection and Public
Library of Detroit; the Rev. John Youse of Pine
Grove and others. I am especially indebted to Mrs.
Howard A. Brinton of Wallingford and Arnold P.
Pilling of Wayne University for their counsel.

Finally I want to thank three friends who lent their warm aid and support: Clarence E. Shaffner of Detroit for his indefatigable efforts to find certain material; Walter D. Edmonds, the novelist, who generously shared from his wide knowledge of the early history of the state of New York; and Paul A. W. Wallace, Pennsylvania historian, who kindly read the manuscript and made invaluable contributions and suggestions.

C. R.

A COUNTRY

OF STRANGERS

◆ *i* ◆

THE girl in gray deerskins was fifteen, perhaps older, she wasn't exactly sure. She couldn't remember, was she four or five when she had been taken? Just that it was Pooxit, the Month of Falling Leaves. Before that there were only red clouds in her mind. Sometimes the clouds thinned a little, not much, barely enough to make out strange forms behind them. One was a house of pink stones all the same shape and size, a house far bigger than her

3

own Indian bark cabin. And sometimes faintly
shining through the mist she thought she could make
out a face with yellow hair piled on top such as
never had she laid eyes on here among the coarse
black heads of her Indian people.

She saw the face with yellow hair clearly the day
they brought the news from the Forks of the Muskingum. The word flew like Tskinnak, the blackbird,
among the cabins of the village. It was that the Lenni
Lenape must give up all children who had once been
white, captives taken in raids across the Ohio and
adopted into the tribe, even those who had married
Indians, and their children. The white captain at
the Forks had decreed it. He had come into the Indian forest with more warriors than leaves on a tree.
Should the Indians refuse, his army would never
depart but settle here in the heart of the Indian
country, cutting down the Indian forest, shooting
the Indian game, and growing like a white cancer in
the breast of the red man.

Memories long buried in Stone Girl's mind rose
up to trouble her. They were the words of Never
Laugh, the white woman captive taken on the same
raid as she. That was when Stone Girl had been very
small and not long here. Never Laugh would take
her into the forest. There in a small patch of sun-

light she would talk to her in the white tongue, first
bringing out pale scraps of dried scalp from her
dress. It was all she had left of her own little girl.
The child had cried too much on the long way to
the Waldhoning, she said, and Fish Spear had
dashed her head against a rock. Never Laugh would
stroke the pitiful shreds of pale hair and cry. Afterward she would put them away, get out her comb,
and comb the Indian lice from Stone Girl's head.

"You must remember, Mary, who you are," she
would say. "Not Stone Girl, daughter of Feast
Maker and granddaughter of Machilek, but Mary
Stanton, daughter of Captain Peter Stanton, assemblyman and friend of the proprietaries in Pennsylvania."

"I am Mary," Stone Girl would answer obediently
but in her mind she would say, "I am Stone Girl,
too."

"They will try to make you a savage," Never
Laugh would go on. "They want you to be a squaw.
When you are older, young men will stand in the
path waiting for you when you go to the spring.
Do not stop and talk but walk around them. They
look harmless enough. Oh, you would never guess
the Indian warrior from what he is here in the village. He furnishes deer meat for his family. He

sits and smokes like the most peaceful of men. When he walks, it is slow like a king. Hardly ever does he raise his voice and when he talks it's as if butter would not melt in his mouth. But it's different out on a war party. Then he turns into a wolf."

"Not my father?"

"Not Captain Stanton, your white father. Oh, a few white men in the woods run wild and do things they would never do at home. Other white men would punish them if they did. But for Indians, savagery is second nature. At home they are the kind husband and sympathetic father. On the war trail they do cruel things I do not want to speak to you about. It is best for you not to know, for you must live with Machilek, your grandfather, since your Indian father is dead, and you must never show fear. But don't forget what I have told you."

"I will remember," Stone Girl would say but in her heart she did not believe such words about Feast Maker, her father, or Machilek, only about Fish Spear who had dashed Never Laugh's child against a stone.

"They will work on you every day," Never Laugh would warn her. "You are young and strong. Just the kind they want. An Indian likes nothing better than to get a white squaw. It makes him feel important among his fellows. The time is coming when I won't be here to remind you. When I'm gone you must remember. Keep your white tongue alive. Talk English every day to yourself and never give up."

Had she given up? Stone Girl asked herself. Well, she had, she reckoned, after Never Laugh died. While the white woman lived it was not too hard to think that perhaps she, Stone Girl, was white also. But once the white woman had been put in the ground, her words had gone into the ground, too. Besides, her grandfather, Machilek, had reminded her who she was.

"You must not believe what Never Laugh tells you," he had said. "She is white. She has never been made one of us. She is too old to be adopted. She is tied by dead vines to white ways. She can understand nothing of the red people. But you are different. You are young and have become our daughter and granddaughter. You understand us. You speak our words and breathe our air. You are one of us. You are Lenni Lenape, the original people."

Then it was a fierce joy for Stone Girl to think and know she was Indian.

"I am Lenni Lenape, too," the blue-eyed son of Munache the Badger told her. "I will never go back to the Yengwe devils. And no one can make me."

But back he went in the hands of his father and uncles to the white captain, and Stone Girl felt the blood in her veins run slow. What would happen to her and her child, Otter Boy, now?

"Is my life to go from here?" she asked Espan, her husband. "And that of your son and likeness?"

"Do not let such in your head," he answered. "Never will I give you and Otter Boy to the white captain."

"Then I stay?" Stone Girl said, and a great joy seized her, for Espan was a man of honor and long experience against the white man.

"You will stay," he agreed. "But first you must go from the village. My friend Smashed Head is one of the Shawanose where the sun sets in summer and is not bound by the white captain. I will ask him and his wife to keep you and Otter Boy. When the white captain leaves, I will bring you back to my cabin. But of this you must breathe to no one."

"I will not breathe," she promised, but in her heart fresh despair seized her. So she was to be taken away after all? What difference did it make to be dragged toward the setting or the rising sun? Either way she and her child would be torn from Espan and her home village.

♦ *ii* ♦

It was deep in the pit of night when they left the cabin.

"Now tread with a light foot," Espan instructed her.

She knew what he meant, not the light foot that goes with a light heart. No, even with a heavy heart and the burden of her child on her back, her foot must crack no stick on the ground. None in the

village dare hear them go and say that Espan had
disobeyed orders of the white captain. She must
simply disappear. Then if the white soldiers came
looking for her and Otter Boy, all that anyone in
the village could tell was that one day Stone Girl
and her small son were here and the next day the
earth had swallowed them up.

It was true enough, Stone Girl told herself as
they went. The earth was swallowing them up. Not
even Getanitowit, He Who Is Above All, she
thought, could peer down through the darkness and
see her being taken away. At this bewitched hour
nothing looked familiar. The path was a will-o'-the-
wisp, the trees they passed under, phantoms.
Strange bushes stood in the form of unknown beasts
and opened their mouths at her as she went by. All
she knew was that they tramped into the teeth of
Lomache, the north wind, which blew from the Place
of Dancing Wraiths far from the home village on
the Waldhoning, or White Woman's River.

From the beginning, the omens were not good.
When daylight came, they passed old scalps hanging from a tree beside their path. The hair swayed
dismally in the breeze. The following day they
reached Smashed Head's village. Dogs tried to tear
them apart and nobody called them off. At Smashed

Head's cabin his wife said he was away in council with the Northward Indians and nobody knew, not even he himself, when he would be back. Espan asked for Smashed Head's brother but he was gone, too. For a time, Espan stood thwarted, flicking no eyelash, waiting, reserved and proud. Then he went through the ceremony with Smashed Head's wife, presenting his gift of strouding for her husband, telling her of his mission, reciting Stone Girl's merits as a worker, and at the end announcing he must be back in his own village before the white soldiers came.

Stone Girl felt a sinking when he gave her and Otter Boy farewell. He was going home without them. She stood outside this unaccustomed cabin with her child in her arms and watched his figure depart, moving into the forest until he passed from sight and she could make out nothing more among the trees. But the rest of the day her mind went with him on the path, passing the places they had seen together, lying at night under the same high bank for warmth, all the time coming closer to the home village. At last she could see him on the familiar path climbing the yellow bluffs and now he reached their snug cabin. But their fire would be out, their bed cold, and the cabin lifeless without

Otter Boy. Espan would have to go to his brother,
Slow Day, for flame to warm him and something
to eat.

The night was long and yet when morning came
Stone Girl could sing to her son a little tune. The
Indian words were meaningless but the air said, "It
is all right now, Little Mouse. Night has passed. So
will the long winter. The ugly white captain will go.
The handsome red father will come. We must only
endure like the stone."

Then Smashed Head arrived home. He looked
stern when he found Stone Girl and Otter Boy. As
a Shawano his tongue was different but Stone Girl
could understand him.

"Daughter," he told her, "Espan should have
waited. I could have given him instructions. Not
only the Lenni Lenape but the Shawanose must give
up their white sons and daughters. The word has
been spoken. Daughter, you are not safe here. If you
don't go back to the Yengwe, I must take you to the
Northward Indians. There you can hide under a
bush till the storm blows over."

They left in the morning. The first journey had
been hard enough. It had not been easy to sever the
green vines that had bound her to the village so
long. She had felt herself a bush torn up by the

roots and thrown away to wither. But that going
away had been preferable to this. Then her husband
had journeyed with her. He had led her to the lodge
of his friend and when he left had promised soon to
return for her. Now she had to journey with a
stranger, to be led by him to an unknown land of
strangers somewhere at the ends of the earth. What
would happen to her and Otter Boy there nobody
knew.

That night with her back to the trunk of a huge
sycamore and her child in her arms she dreamed that
a great white bird flew over her head calling her
name. But when she answered and ran out there
was nothing but a white mist through dead vines
swinging back and forth in the wind like the hair of
the ancient scalps they had seen on the way from
Mahonink. Next day they came to a shaking asp
grove with limbs bare to the sky where she raised a
silent voice to Him Who Is Above All.

"Here I go again. I am Stone Girl and this is my
son!" she called. "Can you see us being taken
away?" But nothing flew over her head but Waapalane, the bald eagle, and there was no answer, except once she thought she heard the great bird
scream.

In the afternoon she and Smashed Head reached

the Long Path. Turn to the right on it, and she knew it would take her back close to Espan and the home village. Smashed Head turned to the left.

"Nocha, Father," she asked, "can you tell me where we go now?"

But all he would tell her was that the path led to the Great Sweet Water, adding the names of nations that had tramped it, the Northward Indians, whom the Yengwes called Wyandots and the Plantsche-man called Huron, who were the strong friends and allies of the Shawanose although they had no blood ties between them and spoke a different tongue, so that they needed an interpreter together. The Mi-amis also knew the path, and their cousins, the Picts or Pickwaulines, who lived at Pickawillany on the Sciota, where they called the Lenni Lenape grand-fathers and could speak to them without a go-be-tween. Other feet on the path had been those of the Ottawas and Chippeways of the north wind; the Puttowatomies, who lived west of the Star That Did Not Move; the Illinois, the We'as, the Kickapoos and Plankeshawes, who ate serpents. Even some of the faraway Fox had tramped it, as had the Sauk and Menominees, the Conesdagas and Cochnawagas, the Abrakies, Oswegatchies, and Meposages. Smashed Head recited the names of tribes she had never heard of, the Mascoutens, Peanguieseins, the Paccouarias, Ayouz, Sioux, and Tintons, rolling the strange names over his tongue as if they gave him strong pleasure. But they gave Stone Girl dull despair. These were the Echokike, the ends of the world, to which she was being taken. Home had become no more than a dream behind her.

Another day and the girl found the hills failing under her feet. The next afternoon they came to a desolate place where no trees would grow. On the far side of the barrenness lay a cheerless village. The cabins stood unlike any Stone Girl had ever seen before. The river flowed north instead of south. And the people spoke a language unintelligible as that of the jay and the gray wolf. Only when they brought out the strangest thing of all, a white man with gold lace on his red coat, did she catch any of the words. He was the interpreter, the bridge between the two nations, and now she heard Smashed Head tell him to recite to the village people all the good things Espan had told Smashed Head's wife about Stone Girl and the work she could do. There was much palavering. She saw Smashed Head leave with a deerskin sack of corn on his back. Then a Northward Indian with a silver skewer in his nose took her to his cabin, where a woman lay stiff with the Sick-

ness That Freezes Joints. Here she was ordered
with signs what to do.

What was she now? Stone Girl asked herself that
night when allowed to lie down and rest. Was she
a prisoner again to be made over in the image of
her captors? It had not been hard when she was very
young and pliable like the wands of the willow. But
she was no small child any more. And how could she
be a prisoner if she were still Indian? Had she become white again or perhaps black like the slave in
the village below Mahonink? His owner, Three Suns,
used to dress him in a long shirt of vermilion strouding and march him up and down the village behind
him like a squaw. Had she been Indian, she specu-
lated, the Great Spirit of the Indians would not
have forsaken her. And if she were white, the white
trader in a red coat and gold lace would not have
stood indifferently by while one of his own race was
bargained for like a blanket in his post. No, she
must be black now and a slave, she reasoned.

The following day the trader accosted her from
his post door in the language of Never Laugh, which
Stone Girl barely remembered.

"Can you understand me?" he asked, and when
she nodded slowly, "Do you want to get out of here?
Then listen. When they show you how to do any-

thing, you must do it badly. When they teach you their language, you must say the words wrong. You must be stupid in everything, but don't tell them I said so."

"I could never do that," Stone Girl told him.

"Then you will stay here till hell freezes over," the trader said, turning away, and Stone Girl lay awake half the night pondering.

This was the hardest thing she had ever taken on herself to do, to make her hands spoil good hide and meat, and her tongue words that her ears heard plainly enough. It was harder still to see the faces of disgust and the flash of anger in Indian eyes. But the worst was the way they treated Otter Boy. When she first came he had almost been as one of their own. Now they scorned and abused him. Hardly could she have carried on except for the trader in gold lace.

"You're doing fine. Keep up the good work," he would say in Yengwe when he passed her. "It won't be long now."

And that was the way she thought it was working out when a white man in a black robe came up the river in a strange kind of boat. He carried in his hands two golden sticks crossed and fastened together. A charm of the same design hung around his neck. He set up a kind of table of boughs and stood in front of it doing incomprehensible acts and singing words in an incomprehensible tongue while the Indians watched gravely.

When it was over the Indian with a skewer in his nose talked with him, after which he brought him to see Stone Girl and Otter Boy. Then all went to the trader's log house, where Black Robe and the Indian kept lifting bar lead, rings, combs, looking glasses, and scissors as they spoke, and she knew she was being traded for again, like one of the scalping knives on the log counter.

"Now you are free," the trader told her in English when it was done.

But when she took Otter Boy and started for home on the path by which she had come, they ran after and stopped her. She couldn't do that. She must stay with Black Robe now. He had paid for her. She and Otter Boy belonged to him, and now she had to stand while he put water on Otter Boy's head and spoke outlandish words from a talking book in his hand. She told herself that he must have some design on her child's shiny black hair, and that night when she and Otter Boy slept in the post with the smell of raw furs and the dye of cloth and other alien objects in their nostrils, her hands felt up on the log counter where she had seen a pair of trade scissors. Then she snipped off the Indian locks close to his soft head.

"Now he will find it hard to scalp you, Little Mouse," she promised.

Next morning she was told to carry him into the long boat, not like the elm-bark canoe or heavy like the hollowed tree, but made of wide strips of wood fastened together and waterproofed with the hardened black sap of the Tree That the Lightning Likes to Strike. Instead of paddlers there were stout hairy men who spoke the same tongue as the man with the black robe and sang as they pulled on their wooden handles.

"Smile. You don't know how lucky you are," the trader in gold lace called after her when the boat pushed off.

But how could she smile? The boat was headed not south but north. Every minute it moved still farther into the unknown, away from the beloved Waldhoning and home. The river grew wider. She could see in front of them a frightening expanse of water. As they passed the last land, water lay to the east and water to the west while to the north stretched such a watery waste she could see nothing but waves as when from a hill she looked down on the green forest in a summer storm.

Presently the boat turned away from the rising

sun, where Never Laugh had said that her mother
with the yellow hair lived, and moved toward the
sun's setting, where according to Smashed Head
lived only foreigners like the Sauks and Fox and the
faraway Sioux, who hunted the herds of the black
bulls. She would not tell Otter Boy but in her own
heart she had given up all hope. The white trader
with gold lace had betrayed her. Getanitowit had
washed his hands of her, for how could the Great
Spirit have anything to do with a white man in a
black robe like a woman, with two crossed sticks on
his breast and his home in a nation of barbarous,
hairy-faced men to whom he was taking her?

STONE GIRL had liked the sound of the words, the
Great Sweet Water, when first she had heard them.
In her mind she had seen a long stretch of river, like
looking down the Waldhoning to the far bend where
a canoe on the river was like Damaskus, the muskrat, swimming across. But now the name gave her
fear for this watery world, unstable, desolate, and
never still. Neither muskrat nor otter could be seen
upon it, only their lone boat which the winds tried

to break in small pieces and send to the bottom. Twice the hairy-faced rowers had to put in to a stony beach and wait for Tgui, the waves, to lose their anger. Then one morning the bateaumen started to sing again and not long afterward Stone Girl found the boat in the welcome shelter of a river with solid banks of her mother, Earth, on both sides.

"Little Mouse, we don't drown after all," she whispered. "I think that maybe we go home now. Little Mouse, your Guka, mamma, has heard the Muskingum is wide like this where it empties into the Beautiful River."

But her hopes withered when she saw fields and more fields. The Muskingum never could have had so many. Now the hairy-faced bateaumen raised their voices lustily and coming around the bend she saw a frightening sight, a white man's town with a high fence of upright poles around it. Strange off-the-ground cabins perched above the four corners and gate, and inside the stockade were the steep pitched roofs of curious houses with snow lying white upon them like on a hundred hills and gullies.

At a small village on the other side of the river Black Robe took her and Otter Boy into a long house where a sour-eyed woman with a red kerchief on her head listened to what he told her. The sour-eyed woman spoke to Stone Girl, but how could she answer when she understood not a word, only the shrugs and grimaces? She guessed the woman had little use for her and less for Otter Boy, for she kept throwing up her hands. In the end Black Robe took them in a canoe which he himself paddled across the river.

Otter Boy whimpered as they headed toward the frightening town and towers on the other side.

"Little Mouse. If they kill you, they must kill me, too," she consoled him. "I will be there to carry you on my back into the Joyous World. Little Mouse. If they wanted to kill us, I think they would have done it already."

The river was alive with boats going here and there, up and down, from one side to the other. It seemed that everybody here went by boat instead of feet, Indians and white, old and young. The rowers that passed close by greeted Black Robe with respect. Some made a curious sign across their breast and forehead. On the bank Black Robe motioned her to follow him and she saw uneasily that they headed toward the gate with a house on top and soldiers with guns looking out.

"Little Mouse, be a warrior now," she told him.

Once inside the gate, hardly could she go on for

the strangeness. The street flowed with people like a river with leaves in the fall, the women in bright reds, purples, and yellows, the soldiers with the rainbow sewn in their coats. Only the Indians in blankets and matchcoats reassured her, standing around without surprise at the marvel of water-colored iron through which you could see but not reach and the tower of a long house that went up in the sky.

"Little Mouse. Do you see all that I see?" she whispered. "Do you hear the white man's tomahawk that strikes on iron and his long knife that cuts through wood?"

Black Robe took her to the door of a house with an outside room in front, a room whitewashed and without walls on three sides, so that a bird could fly through. It must be the house of a white chief, she thought, for a captain with several Indian chiefs left as they came. Black Robe struck the door with the golden iron that hung on it and a girl like Stone Girl appeared with another red kerchief on her head. She greeted Black Robe in his own Plantscheman tongue, and now Stone Girl felt the first warm melting in her breast, for when they entered, the strange girl fondled Otter Boy with her hand and made gurgling child sounds to him as they passed.

Suddenly in the roofed passageway a strange feeling came over Stone Girl, and at the door to the big room the red clouds she had known as a small girl tried to come swirling around her. She felt sure for a moment she had been here before and soon she must see the lady with yellow hair who had troubled her in her dreams. But the real lady she saw in front of her had hair black as an Indian's. Still so close to the vision that she could bring the red clouds about her again if she wanted, Stone Girl saw Black Robe shake hands with the blackhaired lady and talk to her in the Plantscheman tongue.

The lady turned to Stone Girl and spoke to her in the same language. When Stone Girl did not understand or reply, her voice changed and the girl found her speaking in the tongue of Never Laugh and the trader with gold lace.

"Do you understand me now?" she asked, and when the girl inclined her head, "You are English, then?"

"I am Indian," Stone Girl answered.

"So?" the lady said gravely. "Of what nation are you?"

"I am Lenni Lenape and so is Otter Boy. We are of the Original People that are grandfathers to other nations."

The lady's black eyes snapped and now she spoke to her in Lenni Lenape, not as they spoke it at home but close enough so that Stone Girl could almost feel Espan waiting for her in the village along the Waldhoning.

"You are of the nation that we French call Loups," the lady told her. "You are a long way from home. But before you were Lenni Lenape, you were English, not so?"

"My father, Feast Maker, washed all the English off me when I was little," Stone Girl told her. "Now I am Indian."

"Do you remember where you came from?"

"I come from Mahonink along the Waldhoning, the White Woman's River."

"I mean the English place you came from before that."

The girl was silent. The lady went on.

"I want you to tell me all you remember," she urged quietly, and it was hard for Stone Girl to keep back with the vision only a few moments before.

"I remember nothing," she answered. "Sometimes in a dream I see."

"What do you see, child?"

"I see a house of pink stone. A great house like this."

The lady nodded gravely and spoke to Black
Robe, who nodded, too.

"And what do you remember of your father and
mother? I mean your English father and mother."

"I remember nothing. Sometimes I see a lady like
you but with yellow hair."

"And your father?"

"He never comes in the dream."

"Do you remember the English name?"

"Never Laugh told me. But she is in the ground
and the name is in the ground with her. It is no part
of me any more."

"Did this person, Never Laugh, ever tell you
about your father?"

"Only that he is in the white councils."

"Did she ever say that you should go back to
your white father and mother?"

"She told me. Yes. But that was before I have
Espan, my husband. I am an Indian wife now. I
have an Indian son. How could I go back to the
white people?"

The lady said no more to her but the black eyes
softened in a look that made the girl wonder. The
lady and Black Robe sat talking a long time in the
Plantscheman tongue. Stone Girl could tell little
from their faces. Only from the face of the girl who

had let them in did she catch an inkling. The girl stood listening in the hall out of sight of the lady and Black Robe, her face very sober. As they talked the face of the girl in the hall grew graver till almost it looked cruel. All of a sudden it brightened and she flashed a smile to Stone Girl, a good Indian smile like the sun coming out from under a dark cloud. Then she was gone. Sure enough, the lady and Black Robe were rising now. They shook hands again. Black Robe started to leave and when Stone Girl started after him, the lady stopped her.

"You are staying here with me, child, till we find out who you are and where you belong. Sooner or later everybody comes here, for I am Madame Corbusier, the interpreter for Colonel Gladwin. Father Le Clercq tells me how well you work. Simone will show you what to do and where to sleep. She will teach you the Plantscheman tongue, and I will teach you to remember some of your own English tongue."

She called the girl with the red kerchief, who came in and listened gravely as if she hadn't heard everything before.

Out in the place of pots and pans, Simone gave her a quick pinch like a cousin.

"I am white too once," she chattered. "But now I am Puttowatomi. Puttowatomi is the grandchild of the Lenni Lenape and the language is the same. Can you understand what I say?"

"I can understand a little," Stone Girl said. "Not all, just some, but enough."

"Madame says your name now will be Claire," Simone told her. "It is a good Plantscheman name like mine. For a while I thought that she would not pay Father Le Clercq the price he paid for you. The Plantscheman has no stomach except to buy at the lowest price but he has a good side, too. He doesn't mind that you have an Indian son. The Yengwe hates the Indian but the Plantscheman marries and has children with the Indian. So you be happy now."

◆ *iv* ◆

STONE GIRL didn't know what she would have done
in this strange place without Simone. She taught
Stone Girl to laugh at the outlandish ways of the
white man; at the hard Plantscheman shoes clatter-
ing like horses over the brick floor; at the crazy stairs
which the Plantschemen ran up like squirrels up a
tree; at the choking smell of the small white balls
that Madame Corbusier kept to ward off the evil
spirit of Pitquok, the poor harmless moth, which

the Plantscheman woman feared more than the wolf at the door; and at Nisku, dirt, which she feared still more than the moth, forgetting that dirt was what her mother, the Earth, was made of.

"The white people are very funny, Claire," Simone said. "Their bones are soft like moss and that is why they must have beds of feathers. When first I came I had to lie on the floor to sleep. Now my bones are soft, too, and I can dive between my feather bags like a frog in the mud."

Oh, Stone Girl couldn't help but like Simone. She had the bold Indian humor. She showed Stone Girl how to dip her knees in the Plantscheman fashion when she passed the figure of a woman always standing in a corner downstairs and then to rap it with her knuckles to show it was only wood. When Père Le Clercq came to hold prayers, she caused the time on their knees to go faster by making comical Plantscheman eyes and faces with motions of scrubbing the floor. And when Stone Girl asked why did they have a china face with a tin tongue on the wall, Simone had a ready answer.

"It's the water in the white man's head. You know, Claire, that water is very soft. If you make marks on water they are soon gone and forgotten. Now the Indian head has no water. It is hard like the bark of a beech tree and marks on it will stay as long as he lives. But the watery head of the white man can't remember is it time to eat or go hungry or is it time to go to bed or get up, so he makes himself a machine to remember for him."

"But why does he have it call out to him in the middle of the night when he is asleep and doesn't need to remember?" Stone Girl asked.

"Who can explain the white man?" Simone said. "He wants to know everything even when he is asleep."

The Snow Month passed, after that the Month When the Trees Crack with Cold and the Month When the Ground Squirrel Looks Out on the World. It was plain that the snow season was getting old. Tocu, the cold, could be seen creeping out of the ground, and the Season of New Leaves hung ready to drop from the sky. In her mind Stone Girl could see Espan making his moccasins watertight for his journey to find her. When the Month of Many Fish Bones arrived, she felt sure he was on his way.

But the summer passed. Espan did not come and Stone Girl would have gone around like Tschipey, a ghost, if it had not been for Simone. Daily Simone filled her head with other notions including the peculiar sounds of the Plantscheman tongue that

went up on the end like the tail of a cat. By fall
Stone Girl knew it well enough to listen and understand when Simone was called into the front room.
She heard Père Le Clercq tell Simone he had brought
Madame Corbusier a letter from a brother priest at
the other end of the Great Sweet Water. The brother
priest had found Simone's white father, a miller, in
the Dutch province of New York, who had lost her
to the Indians. Madame Corbusier was much moved
when she told Simone that Père Le Clercq would
take her home.

"I have a home here," Simone protested quickly.
"I don't need another."

"Hush, child," Madame Corbusier reproved her.
"You must go to your poor parents who have
mourned you all these years."

"I know you, Madame Corbusier," Simone de-
clared with vigor. "I know Claire and Otter Boy.
But I do not know these people you and Père Le
Clercq talk about. They are nothing to me."

"Do not speak such impiety, Simone," Madame
Corbusier admonished. "God in his Holy Writ de-
clares you must honor your father and your
mother."

"You are my mother, Madame Corbusier," Simone
said. "If you chase me out, I must go, but not to

this faraway place of the foreign Yengwe who are enemies of the Indian and Plantscheman and where I am a stranger."

Père Le Clercq stepped forward.

"We will hear no more of this, Simone," he said sternly. "I have already written a letter for the sloop *Fairness* to take back. In this letter, I have promised to return you to the father and mother that God gave you."

"Then you will have to tie me up like a lynx on a pole," Simone told him. "And like you I make a promise that I will bite and scratch all the way."

Madame Corbusier rebuked her but Stone Girl, peering in from the other room, saw her and Père Le Clercq exchange glances. They talked together privately in the Huron tongue.

"Simone," the lady announced. "I am as loath to lose you as you are to leave. Winter is almost upon us. Ice will soon stop the boats. We have decided to wait until spring. That will give you time to grow accustomed to the idea."

"Madame Corbusier, next spring my teeth and fingernails will be just as sharp," Simone promised.

Next spring came and it was plain that Madame had not given up her resolve. She had Simone show Stone Girl all the Plantscheman dishes that Madame

Corbusier had taught Simone to prepare. And to make Stone Girl more fluent in Plantscheman words, she said that the girls must speak no longer in their Indian tongue, not even in the privacy of their sleeping room. They would have no need of Lenni Lenape words where they were going anyhow. It was not easy for the two girls to shut off the beloved language. When they felt they had to say something to each other in Indian now, they said it to Otter Boy in the other's hearing. To keep Indian words alive in their breasts they told Otter Boy long stories in the same tongue.

"This happened a long time ago when the whole world was dark" one story began. "The darkness was very unhandy. Woakus, the gray fox, could not tell if he was gray or black, and Wulalow, the One with the Beautiful Tail, could not see if he had a tail at all. Tshimalus, the bluebird, had never looked on his bright blue wings, and Skaak, the polecat, could not admire his handsome white stripe. Many accidents happened. Memeu, the woodcock, flew into a tree and broke his wing so he had to go on the ground and drag it like Pachquachus, the mouse, his tail. Hunja, the bull that butts with his head, bumped into Nunscheach, the she-bear, and that was a mighty snarling and roaring. The only one

that didn't have an accident was Ssappis, the lightning bug, for he carried his torch in his breast."

She stopped as she always did at this point and
asked if she should tell more.

"Bischi!" Otter Boy gurgled, which meant yes,
surely, and was the nearest the Indian tongue came
to the Plantscheman s'il vous plaît, if you please,
or je vous en prie, I beg of you, for the Indian
would not even beg for his life and had no begging
word in his language.

"One day," Stone Girl went on, "Kwal, the blue
jay, flew into the face of Long Tail, the panther. A
terrible quarrel followed that could be heard all
through the forest. Long Tail screamed at the blue
jay and the blue jay at Long Tail and when they
had called each other all the bad names they could
think of, they called bad names for their mothers
and fathers and grandmothers and grandfathers.
The animals gathered around and shook their heads.
This was unbrotherly. Something had to be done.
Memakockus, the red-headed woodpecker, told how
he could roll up a ball of the inner bark of Wipun-
quok, the white oak, fastened together with pitch
from the Tree That the Lightning Likes to Strike.
Woapink, the possum, who is very wise, showed
them how to strike flint to get a spark to light it.

Then all the animals blew on it and Achto, the deer, who is very fast, ran with it through the forest till it was a ball of fire. When he got back, Waapalane, the eagle, was waiting to take it up in the sky higher than any other could go, and it has been up there giving us light ever since and now we call it the father of us Indians."

Generally when she finished the story, Otter Boy would run to the window to look out and try to see the ball of fire. Since it was night he would come back disappointed and ask Simone for her story of the thunders.

"A long time ago there was a white man," Simone began. "Now most white men are foolish but this one most of all, for he wanted to find the place where the thunders lived. He went westward and westward till he passed the place of the setting sun. Here he saw a high mountain. The top was covered with clouds. The trees on the side of the mountain were split in pieces and stripped of bark, so he knew he had come to the dwelling place of the thunders. He climbed on through the clouds till he found a nest as big as a house and in it a brood of young thunders not yet ready to fly. Around the nest were the skeletons of serpents the old thunders brought the young to eat. The foolish white man thought he would

take one of the young thunders back to show to his
people. He reached in with his spear but the young
thunders gave a loud clap of alarm. Fire flashed
from their mouths. The spear was shattered in
pieces and the white man's arm broken so that it
hung like the neck of a slain snipe. Far away he
heard the old thunders answer. They had heard the
call of their young and were coming back to the
nest. The white man tried to run down off the mountain but the old thunders were too fast for him.
They struck him to the ground with their fire
and there he lies, burned black as pitch, to this
day."

Otter Boy had been sitting on the floor drinking
in the good Indian words. Now he asked Simone
for another story and she told him her favorite.

"A long time ago a Puttowatomi girl was born in
the beech forest," she began. "Her mother looked
up and saw a small girl in the village playing with
her father's war paint, so she called her baby Red
Girl. It was a powerful name and when Red Girl
grew up she was shapely and strong with the red
color always in her cheeks. Many Puttowatomi young
men tried to talk to her but she would talk to only
one and after that they were always seen together.
But one day he went to war and never came back,

and now all the color began to fade out of Red Girl's
cheeks. She would scarcely eat or speak and at last
He Who Is Above All looked down and saw her.
Where are those pretty red cheeks I liked? he asked.
Something must be done. So he changed her into
a bird to fly to her missing lover in the Joyous Land
That Is Beyond Our Sight. But she still looked
pale to the Great Spirit. How would her lover know
her? So he took the red that used to be on her cheeks
and put it on her breast. Then she flew away to the
distant region, promising her friends not to stay
but to come back in the spring. And every year when
the ice goes out of the river, she keeps her promise.
You can see her red breast and hear her telling her
friends that she is back."

Of late this story had made Stone Girl sad. She
would sit very quiet thinking of Espan and pondering why he had never come for her. Surely Smashed
Head would have told him to what village of the
Northward Indians he had taken her, and surely the
Northward Indians would have told Espan when he
got there that Black Robe had taken her across the
Great Sweet Water. It was a very long way, to be
sure, but that would be nothing for Espan, who had
legs like wings and traveled a long way each year
to fight the Long Knives.

Always Simone would see Stone Girl's sadness and try to cheer her.

"Stone Girl. In my mind I see someone coming," she predicted. "It is a man. He will not even knock. Madame Corbusier's front door will open. You will look up and it will be Espan."

But the Month of the Tree Whose Branches Are Pounded for Baskets passed. The Plantschemen plowed their fields again and dug their gardens. Flowers bloomed once more on the Plantscheman fruit trees and bushes. The Month That Brings the Summer passed and the Month When the Deer Turns Red.

"Perhaps," Simone tried to cheer her, "the great white captain still camps along the Muskingum and Espan can't come till he goes."

But Stone Girl felt in her heart it was not true. The white captain long since must have gone back to the Quekel province. She watched the Month When the Deer Turns Gray pass into the Month of Cool Nights and now the plants in Madame Corbusier's garden began to wither from the first frost.

"He has only lost his way. He will find it again," Simone promised.

But Stone Girl knew that Espan was no white man to get turned around in the woods. He would never foolishly think the sun rose in the west and set in the east. Besides, he was the one to do things quickly as when he had taken her and Otter Boy away from the white captain. One afternoon he had told her and that same night they had gone. No, something must have happened to him, something Machit, ugly. Before the first snow Père Le Clercq brought the gloomy tidings. The priest had been down to baptize and say mass at the village of the Northward Indians. They had told him that Smashed Head had been there asking about Stone Girl. Smashed Head told the trader with gold lace that Espan had gone on a war party against the Long Knives and had never come back. Three from his village had fallen. He did not remember the names of the others but the first to fall had been Espan.

◆ *v* ◆

So ESPAN, her husband, was no more. The strong
heart that had beat so steadily had stopped and his
Tschipey, spirit, gone to Awossajame, the Joyous
Hunting Land, the Place That Is Beyond Our
Sight. Madame Corbusier and Père Le Clercq said
it was up in le ciel, the sky. Stone Girl thought that a
strange place for forests and rivers and jumping
deer. On the other hand, she admitted that more than
once she had seen blue mountains and pearly lakes

42

in the sky as well as the shapes of fish and beasts
and turtles, along with other stranger creatures
whose names she did not know. And everyone knew
that ducks and geese flew into the sky until they
disappeared from view.

Stone Girl remembered that Machilek, her grandfather, had told her the Joyous Hunting Land lay
to the south and west. He said an old friend of his,
Hear Smoke, had once seen it. This was in the time
of famine. Hear Smoke had gone unusually far
hunting Achto, the deer, and had come to where the
earth meets the sky. The two were tightly fitted together, he said, as leggings on a leg, but he found a
place where a boulder had split under the sky's
weight and he could crawl through. Lying there
with his feet in this life and his head in the next, he
could smell the game, could see the deer leap and
hear the pheasant drum. He itched to crawl all the
way through and get a deer to bring home but feared
that then he himself would become a Tschipey,
ghost, and never be able to return. Besides, he said,
the deer of the Joyous Hunting Ground were too
big and fat to be dragged back through the small
hole in which he lay.

Oh, Stone Girl had no misgivings about the good
things in the Place Beyond Our Sight. It was the

bad in this world that troubled her, that Espan had
lost his life far from home in the country of the
Long Knives. Had he been scalped, she wondered,
and forced to go to the Joyous Hunting Ground
without his hair? Had the Long Knives buried him
suitably with rocks on his grave to keep away the
wolves and wolverines? And had they left his gun,
knife, and tomahawk for him to hunt with in the
new land?

She told Otter Boy what had happened and that
was not easy to do. Otter Boy sat listening, blinking
his black eyes. Then he nodded as if to say, now I
know, now you have told me, and went about his
business of playing with the spools Madame Corbusier had given him. That was almost the hardest
part to bear, she told herself, that Espan's own son
did not remember his father, his hawk face or eagle
eyes, his light step on the path, how he sat sagely
with his pipe by the fire or strode out in ceremonial
dress, his ruffled shirt with silver brooches falling
to his knees and his best moccasins stitched in many
colors and decorated with shells.

That was what she had lived for, the day when she
and Otter Boy could return to their protector, their
provider of meat and bringer of joy and booty. How
could she go back now? The green vines that had

bound her to him were broken. The path to his village had grown shut. If ever she went, others would look out of their door to pity her. Otter Boy would run among the cabins looking for his father but never would he find him. When she woke in the early morning, Espan's bed beside her would be empty and cold. She belonged to him no more. She and Otter Boy were alone. Above them the sky had cracked. The rock under their feet had broken. On them wild geese had shaken icy drops from their legs and wings. The morning star had been shot down by arrows. Wherever they went now the fountains would be dried up, the caverns of darkness opened, and the breath in their faces the stale air of yesterday.

Simone tried to wipe the cruel look from Stone Girl's face. She told her the happy story of the time the Chippeways ate the ground hog, who was their own relative since the Indian race had once, like the ground hog, come out of the ground. There were other happy stories, and when they failed, she got down to more solid matters.

"You know, Claire, you are not alone. You still have your sister."

"Sister. I am glad but a sister is not the same. She can't be a father to Otter Boy or give him a baby brother."

"Sister. You yourself can make eyes at one of those bearded voyageurs and soon Otter Boy will have a father."

"Sister. I don't think Little Mouse would like such a hairy face to kiss."

"Madame Corbusier says a kiss without a mustache and beard is like soup without salt and pepper," Simone reminded.

But Stone Girl could not laugh, not even in secret when Madame Corbusier had the gout and looked so comical sitting with her foot on a pink cushion and everybody had to watch out not to touch the cushion or even walk except on tiptoe over the brick floor. Neither did she think it funny when the Madame called for water to mix with the Plantscheman doctor's powders, not asking if it was water scooped upstream or down, for every Indian knows that the former will come up on a sick person like vomit and that the latter will go the other way.

This was the winter that Madame Corbusier was named godmother at the christening of the new church bells and was allowed the honor of taking up the collection dressed in the same silken cloth that draped the bells behind the sanctuary railing. The Saturday before, the two girls had watched her practice the sweeping curtsy she would make after each Plantscheman dropped his or her money into the basket. After supper they had to bathe her, paint and powder her cheeks, and curl her hair. Not a hair must be out of place, and when at last she was all fixed up she dared not go to bed lest she spoil it but sat up all night in her finery till early-morning mass. Simone could hardly wait to get into their own bed, which shook with long-bottled-up laughter, but Stone Girl lay unmoved beside her.

Was this to be her lot from now on? she asked herself. To go through life with heaviness on her heart? The festival came that the Plantscheman called Noël, and the Yengwe, Christmas. Midnight mass at St. Anne's was crowded with residents, soldiers, voyageurs, farmers and their wives all in their brightest colors. Many had to stand outside. On His Majesty's birthday the cannon of the fort roared three times and were answered by the six swivel guns on the sloop. That night gaiety ran through the town. Yengwe officers and Plantscheman ladies came to Madame Corbusier's house to celebrate. But Stone Girl could feel no pleasure in it.

It must be the sickness that came on every woman left alone on the earth, Stone Girl told herself. Even Mardi Gras failed to lift her. Days before, she and Simone had been sent through the fort and countryside with invitations to Madame Corbusier's house for Virez les Crêpes, or the Tossing of the Pancakes. The rooms that evening were crowded. Ladies and gentlemen in their fine dress came out in the kitchen to try their hand. First they held the long handle of the pan while another poured in the batter. Then they heated it over the fire and finally had to toss the pancake up in the air and catch it in the pan when it came down. The higher they tossed, the higher the laurels, the greater the cries of admiration, and if it touched the ceiling that was the acme of perfection. Screams of laughter rang out when a pancake missed and fell to the floor. Pyramids of hot cakes with butter and maple sugar between them were their supper and dancing with music of the fiddle followed.

All was gay until the first stroke of twelve from the clock with the white china face on the wall. Then as if the Plantscheman god himself had shouted down the chimney, all eating, drinking, dancing, and laughter ceased. Stone Girl gazed at the suddenly sobered faces of the guests. One minute they had been lively, filled with lighthearted enjoyment. Now mourning had overtaken them and there would be no more pleasure till the white festival of Pâques, which the Yengwe called Easter.

For the first time she felt a kinship with the white race. She was Indian yet she could see that the Plantscheman people had a heart like hers. Joy of life and of laughter had gone out of them as it had out of her. Like her, they mourned for a young god killed by his enemies and banished to Assowajame, the Place That Is Beyond Our Sight.

♦ *vi* ♦

IT WAS a spring that must have come straight from the Lands of the Great Spirit. Snow went early. Mud dried. The Plantscheman festival called Pâques passed and after that, La Fête-Dieu, which the priest called Corpus Christi. Kaak, the wild goose, passed in great winged prongs overhead. At night Stone Girl had heard them like dogs barking in the sky. It stirred the wild flavor in her blood. Psquall, the frog, called again from the wet places. Michalappotis, the spider, spun his lace. Madame Corbusier sent both girls out to river fields to gather Masgik, greens, for Plantscheman dishes. The south wind blew. The air warmed and Otter Boy romped in the sun.

Siquonk, spring, did something for Stone Girl, poured balsam on the deep wounds. The past was past now. What was, was, and what is, is. Espan, she felt sure, had found content in the Joyous Hunting Ground. She had begun to feel content herself but Madame Corbusier would not let the past die. Ever since she learned of Espan's death, she had pressed Stone Girl with questions about her white origins.

"I am sinning against God and your white mother to keep you here so long," she said firmly. "Now that you lost your Indian husband, we must find your white father."

She had Stone Girl tell again what she remembered of the red clouds and the pink stone house, of the lady with the yellow hair and what Never Laugh had told her. She brought home Yengwe officials from the east to question her, including the great Sir William Johnson, who had given a ball in the colonel's quarters. She hoped that one of them might identify her, but all shook their heads. They said they could make nothing from such a hodgepodge of recollections.

Then one day she fetched a big Yengwe officer from Pennsylvania dressed in a blue coat, a wig, and three-cornered hat. Simone reported she did not like the looks of his eyes when she let him in. They saw too much.

"Remember you are of the tribe of Turtle," she warned Stone Girl in the kitchen. "The turtle has a thick shell. He can draw his head under when others bother him."

"Sister. I can't draw my head from Madame Corbusier."

"No, but you can tell her your mind is Pomi, tallow, and all day you have Wipte, the toothache."

It wasn't long before the Madame called Stone Girl into the front room. Otter Boy went after.

"Ah!" the big Yengwe officer began. "So this is the mysterious white captive of the Lenni Lenape?"

He sat on a heavy Plantscheman chair, leaning back, his legs crossed, a glass of wine in his hand. Stone Girl stood straight in front of him while Madame Corbusier told about her. She had the girl turn to one side to show her profile and to pull back her sleeves to bare her white upper arms.

"Yes, yes." The Yengwe nodded. "I see what you mean. She could be Indian from her face but her inner parts give her away. Unless, of course, unless —have you ever considered that she might be a half-blood?"

"I have seen half-bloods, Major, and even pure-bloods, who could pass for whites so far as their faces were concerned," Madame Corbusier said. "But none of them could show such whiteness of the inner flesh as she."

"Extraordinary!" The visitor nodded. "I see what you mean."

"Besides, she has memories of a white life. Also, there was an older white captive in her village who told her about herself."

"All of this, you understand, madame, might be concocted, or, let us say, imagined," the Yengwe officer pointed out. He turned his pale-blue eyes on the girl. "Tell me, girl, what some of your memories might be. I mean of your former life among our white people."

Stone Girl remembered Simone. She stood silent until Madame Corbusier ordered her to be courteous and answer.

"Monsieur, I forget," she said politely.

"Now, now, don't be afraid of me, girl. I'm no

cannibal. I'm not going to eat you. I'm not even going to accuse you of lying. After all, Madame Corbusier thinks you belong to my own race. I just would like to hear for myself what you remember of the English people. Your father, mother, the house you lived in, everything that comes to your mind."

"Monsieur, I don't remember. My mind today is Pomi, tallow."

"Nonsense. You surely remember something," he insisted.

"Monsieur, I have the toothache," she declared. "It makes me forget."

The great man flushed.

"You can't have forgotten everything," he broke out at her. "Enough of this malingering. Your white friend must have told you your name and about your father. Did you come from the town or country, the mountains, the cleared land or the forest? Did you live near a river?"

Stone Girl did not reply. Madame Corbusier answered for her.

"There was a river, Major. Her older friend talked a good deal about it."

"A wide river?" he inquired.

"It was a very wide river, Claire was told. Hardly

could you see across it. But not a deep river. The
boats were flat and shallow."

"Ah!" said the great man as if that meant something. From this time on he sat in deep thought after
each question. There were many strange things he
wanted to know. Stone Girl stood mostly impassive,
watching his pale-blue eyes, and Madame Corbusier
answered for her when she could. Sometimes he threw
up his head and said, "Ah!" like a hound baying on
the trail. More and more he nodded as if satisfied,
and now when he looked at Stone Girl his face seemed
to hold more respect. In the end he asked a most
curious question. He wanted to know did her father
speak in a loud voice, very loud like a gun?

Stone Girl kept her lips closed but Madame Corbusier leaned forward.

"It's strange, Major, that you should ask that. I
remember Claire told me once what her old friend
Never Laugh had told her. She said that when
Claire's white father gave orders in the kitchen, the
pans hanging on the wall would rattle."

At that the officer jumped to his feet. He looked
tall and overpowering pacing up and down the room.
When he turned to the girl his voice swept all before
it.

"I want you to listen now, child. Did you ever

hear the name of Peter Stanton? Don't tell me you
haven't, because I think you have. Look at me.
Doesn't the name Captain Peter Stanton sound familiar in your ears?"

At the sound of it something happened to Stone
Girl. Far back inside of her she felt a door open.
The woman Never Laugh, long in the ground, came
out. She could feel her comb in her hair and hear her
voice in her ears. Forgotten childhood sensations
flooded her with unaccountable warmth, melting
and thawing. And now she could keep up the pre-
tended lapse of memory no longer. She bowed her
head.

"And the name Susquehanna, of the river?" he
went on relentlessly. "You must remember that,
too?"

She did not raise her head, only formed the name
of the river with her lips.

The big man stood in triumph staring at her.

"I knew it," he said. "For some time now I felt
she could be no other than Peter Stanton's missing
daughter. Her first name, I think, is Mary."

At the name, Madame Corbusier crossed herself.

"Thank God she is of Christian parents then."

"Very much indeed," the officer agreed. "Her
father is assemblyman, innkeeper, and master sur-

veyor for the proprietaries. Mrs. Stanton was originally a Philadelphia lady. She has beautiful flaxen
hair as her daughter remembers. Mrs. Stanton's
father was William Hamilton, who married into the
family of the proprietaries. I stayed with the Captain and his lady in their spacious log inn on the
Susquehanna two or three years ago and heard the
whole tragic story. His daughter was taken by
the savages at five years of age and never recovered.
They pinned great hopes on General Bouquet's ex-
pedition and went to Carlisle to meet the captives
when the general and his army returned. I didn't see
them afterward but I heard that their daughter was
not found among them. The disappointment broke
the mother's health. She believed the hard life of the
savages had killed her daughter."

Madame Corbusier crossed herself again. She
looked at Stone Girl with brimming eyes, then at the
Yengwe officer.

"It is the will of le bon Dieu, Major, that brought
you to Fort Detroit. Indeed, I see the hand of God
in all from the missionary journey of Père Le Clercq
to his bringing Claire to my door. Only one thing
troubles me."

"And what is that?" asked the great man be-
nignly.

"The house of pink stone Claire says she remembers."

"Brick, brick!" the officer exclaimed.

"Yes, of course. I understand that. But you said her father's inn, although very large, is of logs."

"True enough, Madame Corbusier. But the girl was not taken from the inn. She had been on a visit to her grandmother in Philadelphia and was being brought home when attacked and stolen. The houses of Philadelphia, if you have ever been there, are of red brick. Her grandmother's house was of this material and it would likely make a strong impression on a little girl from the frontier."

"It is all clear now." Madame Corbusier wiped her eyes. "You yourself are surely an emissary of le bon Dieu, Major. Everything continues to fall into its place. Another of my girls, Simone, has fought against being returned to her parents alone. Now both girls can go together. One will sustain the other. It will be a great loss to me, for I have grown fond of them both. But it would not be morally right for me to keep them here while their mothers mourn. You look doubtful, Major."

"Not at all. I quite subscribe to your sentiments. I am only puzzled to some extent by this small boy who stands here. It can't be Mary Stanton's child. She's so young and he looks Indian."

"It is her child, Major, and he is Indian indeed," Madame Corbusier assured. "Claire, or Mary as you call her, had an Indian husband in captivity. A very worthy man, I understand. He is dead now."

"I hadn't realized that," the officer said. He looked troubled. "You know, Madame Corbusier, there is the question of Captain and Mrs. Stanton."

"I see no conflict there," Madame Corbusier declared. "They are the grandparents and we all know how devoted grandparents are. Their own blood flows in the child. How could you think otherwise?"

"You are French, madame," he reminded. "We are English."

"You English are human, are you not, Major?" Madame Corbusier exclaimed.

"I hope so," he said humbly, but there were reservations in his eyes.

An evening or two later Madame Corbusier called both girls to the front room. Her bright black eyes looked suspiciously wet.

"I feel I must tell you what has developed. It's sad for me but happy for your parents and you. Père Le Clercq and I have been busy. It is arranged for you to be delivered to the bosoms of your families. The hand of le bon Dieu continues to move in the entire transaction. Already last fall Père Le Clercq was to be recalled for discussions with the superiors of his society in Montreal. He couldn't leave the parish but Père Beaujeau has since been sent to relieve him and serve as an assistant when he returns. Père Le Clercq had expected to take the sloop *Michigan* but now he will engage a bateau and experienced bateaumen to take you all first to the province of Colonel Johnson, then to Pennsylvania. Your parents will not be taxed any more than what I paid for your freedom and the transportation, of course, to your homes. Only after you have been safely delivered to your families will Père Le Clercq travel north to Montreal, where I'm sure his superiors will suitably reward him."

The two girls stood there bleakly.

"Madame Corbusier. What would you do without us?" Simone begged.

"I shall miss you," the Madame promised tearfully. "But God has taken pity on me. He has supplied me with a woman, Marie Joseph Goyau, who will take your place. She is of the Muskrat French but is very good, I am told, with the iron and frying pan. With God's help I shall survive."

The two girls said nothing now. Words would have stuck in their throats. But that night in the privacy of their room they consulted together rebelliously and when the white-faced clock on the dining-room wall struck twelve, they crept downstairs. Simone bore two bundles of their belongings. Stone Girl carried Otter Boy, who was asleep. They could hear Madame Corbusier breathing heavily from the open door to her room. Simone unlatched the front door. The streets of the fort were empty and they moved swiftly without being accosted. Only when they reached the portal to the stockade did they find trouble. The heavy gates were closed.

"Open for us!" Simone called, pounding on the great movable posts.

A soldier of the Yengwe garrison leaned from the redoubt above.

"What are you two girls doing out at this time of night?" he wanted to know.

"We go on a mission. We have no time to lose," Simone said.

"What kind of mission and who for?"

"It is a very secret mission."

"I've no doubt," the soldier said sarcastically. "But I can't let you through till you tell me."

"Call your officer, soldier!" Simone demanded.

"And get abused for waking him for two servant girls? Not me," said the soldier. "Be off now. Come back by daylight and the gates will be open."

The two girls turned back reluctantly but they did not give up. They tried other points in the stockade, finding the huge fence of posts too high to climb over. Finally a guard on the wall heard them in the darkness and fired his musket. In the end they went back defeated to the house, where the door remained unlocked.

"The air is that of a tomb and a prison," Simone whispered. "I cannot breathe again till I am safe in the forest."

"Sister. We will try tomorrow by daylight," Stone Girl promised.

But the garrison soldier at the gate had recognized them in the lantern light and told about it. Père Le Clercq was summoned and closeted with Madame Corbusier. The next night a Plantscheman bateauman sat outside either door to the house. The fourth morning both girls, with Otter Boy, were taken aboard a prepared bateau which all too soon cast off from the dock and started down the river on its long journey. Madame Corbusier and Père Beaujeau waved from shore but only Père Le Clercq answered.

"Our life is finished now," Simone said in their Indian tongue.

"We will never give up," Stone Girl promised. "Once we are off this floating bastille and the jailers are gone, we will tie up Père Le Clercq with the cord from his black robe and take our freedom."

◆ *vii* ◆

ALL the way down the river and on the Great Sweet
Water beyond they watched and waited for a time
of escape, whispering together, thinking of little
else but how could they run away with Tgui, the
waves, all around them? On shore Père Le Clercq
kept his sharp eyes on them like Meechgalane, the
hawk, letting no more than one into the bush at a
time. The portage was long and the two girls pressed

against each other as they passed the fearful sight
and sounds of Niagara.

"How can we ever go back now?" Simone
mourned. "Even a fish could not swim up the thun-
dering waters."

"No, but a fox can run through the forest," Stone
Girl reminded her.

And now they laid eyes on another stretch of
Great Sweet Water that Père Le Clercq called Lac
Ontario. Here the bateaumen took them to sea again.
Later they went up a small river that the priest
after consulting his map called Oswego. From a
Lesser Sweet Water, they ascended a still smaller
stream, then portage to a river that grew gradually
larger, passing farms and villages. Père Le Clercq
said the waterway joined another river that emptied
into the Great Salt Water but they would not go so
far, not even to the falls ahead. They turned off
into a creek by a fort and then onto a smaller stream
with a dam and two houses. Père Le Clercq had been
consulting with people along the way in his curious
English pronunciation, and now he informed Simone
that both houses belonged to her parents and that one
was a mill. Simone, who had of late become spirited
and defiant again, grew desperate.

"Ekih! How can I meet these strangers? Let us
jump out and run!" she begged Stone Girl.

"Sister. You will live afterward," Stone Girl told her. "It is not as bad as Angelik, death."

"If they put their foreign faces close to mine to kiss like the Plantscheman, I will let out Allamuin, the scalp yell." Simone promised.

"Sister. Otter Boy and I will help you with Allamuin, the scalp yell. Then maybe they will not come too close."

Both girls huddled in the bateau looking at the scene before them. On the lower side of the mill, water from a turning wheel flashed in the sun. From inside came a continuous roaring like a small Niagara. White dust fine as snow drifted out of the door.

"Sister. What do I do now?" Simone asked.

"It is Gasca, the gauntlet," Stone Girl said. "You will have to run through."

A man had come out of the mill door to gaze at the boat, a little man very active for his age, his clothing covered with white dust which could not hide his apple-red cheeks. He stood peering at the approaching bateau, then ran like a youth to the house. In a moment he came out, a woman with him, a plump older woman with a white apron like Madame Corbusier sometimes wore when guests came.

"Sister," Stone Girl said, "she looks fat and jolly like Ohum, the Indian grandmother."

"Maybe she is Piwitak, the aunt," Simone guessed.

"No, she looks down at you with love like Guka, the mother. Sister, don't call Allamuin, the scalp yell, to her."

Stone Girl, in the bateau with Otter Boy, watched everything. The grandmotherly woman with the man beside her, came slowly down the bank. Her soft brown eyes shone at Simone, whom the priest had ordered out of the boat. She did not try to hug or kiss her, just took her hand and held it in both of hers while she looked at her with wet eyes. Then she came to the boat and took Stone Girl's hand, too, welcoming her, giving her the same steady smile. Stone Girl could smell the motherly smell that came from her.

Simone held back as they all went up to the house together.

"Must I go in with them?" she begged to Stone Girl.

"Sister. She is nice. She is the Guka, mamma."

"She cries!" Simone protested. "Why does she cry when I still breathe?"

"It's the strange custom of the Yengwe," Stone Girl said. "Never Laugh told me that when they are happy they cry."

It was like at Madame Corbusier's in the house

except that now they were not Allogagani, servants.
No, they were honored guests. Not for a moment
was either girl allowed to do anything. They were
made to sit at the table while the old mother stood
over them saying that their inner parts must be
empty after such a long journey and they must
taste this and eat more of that. The father had sent
a mill boy out at once on a horse with the news and
presently the house was filled with older sisters who
hugged Simone and brothers who pumped her hand
up and down and children who stared at her admir-
ingly, called her Aunt Simone, and plagued her with
questions about the Indians.

Afternoon and evening Stone Girl could see Simone looking about her, wondering, puzzling. Is this
all mine? her eyes said. Does this belong to me? Am
I part of it, this house and the life in it, this Guka,
mother, this Nocha, my father; these brothers and
sisters, nephews and nieces? That night in bed with
Stone Girl she tried to be her old rebellious self.

"Sister. We will run off together like I said but
not right away," she promised.

Stone Girl assented but in her heart she felt it
would never happen now. Oh, lying here in the
strange bed Simone made light of her own sisters
and brothers and of their foolish wives and husbands,

but Stone Girl guessed it was only to comfort the other, to try to make believe that nothing had changed. She kept calling Stone Girl sister, as of old, but the other knew with sober wisdom that now it was just a name. For all these years Simone had been a stranger among strangers, an exile in an alien land. Now suddenly she had reached home, the first she had ever known, with blood sisters and brothers, with a real Guka and Nocha, and Nilum in plenty, all with the same flesh as hers, and Stone Girl had become just Nitschu, friend.

"Sister," Simone said, "I am glad you told me not to give Allamuin, the scalp yell. The Great Spirit would not like me to frighten the Guka, mother."

Stone Girl did not blame her. She was a Guka, mamma, herself. She could feel Nichenos, friendship, in this house. Peace lay under it. Peace lay above it. Peace surrounded it. Awaking next morning, it was the same. Birds sang. The sky arched overhead. Grass greened. Cows grazed. A horse stuck his slow head out of the stable door. Fruit trees waited with their fruit. The stream ran. The water wheel turned. The mill hummed. Farmers came bringing sacks of grain on their horses' backs. The farmers sat and talked with the snowy dust faintly sifting over them.

Otter Boy loved it in the mill, going down gravely with Simone's father and sitting still as a mouse in the chair he was lifted in, his black eyes darting at the moving belts and wooden wheels and cogs, his coal-black hair whitening in the floury rain.

It was a hard day when they left but Père Le Clercq was impatient. He had the gold now that Simone's father had paid for her return. The sun shone warm and yet it was like a day of Elmowank, winter, to Stone Girl. Otter Boy did not want to go. The two girls stared at each other.

"How will we breathe parted from each other?" Simone cried.

"I will carry you in my thinking," Stone Girl said, hardening herself.

Simone's mother gave her good-bye with sad eyes.

"I would not let you go except for your mother waiting," she said. "I know how she looks down the path for you."

From the mill they went back to the river named for the Sankhicani or Gunlock people that the whites called Mohawks. Now they worked their way upstream to a village where a wagon took them over a stumpy road to a lake they had not seen before where men and women from the German settlements were leaving to start a new life in the Quaker province. Stone Girl could understand nothing they said nor the talk of Indians they met along the way. At first logs clogged the stream but creek after creek swelled the small river until they floated easily at last on a broad bosom of water that took them by an old Indian town, then through endless, high, wooded hills and finally rugged mountains.

"Guka, Mamma. The people here must be very bad," Otter Boy said. "Lennau, look! how the Great Spirit makes the earth hard and rough for them to travel on."

"Otter Boy. I have heard of this place," Stone Girl told him. "It is the white people who are bad, not our Indian people."

Next afternoon another river, broad as their own, joined them from the west and now the river flowed very wide.

"Guka, Mamma. Why do we stop when it is not yet night?" Otter Boy asked.

"Otter Boy. This must be the place," Stone Girl told him. "Never Laugh said it was where you could not see if a man or woman stood on the other side."

When they climbed the steep bank, Stone Girl saw open fields and houses in a broad valley. As she

gazed at the scene something came over her and she
stumbled against Otter Boy.

"Guka, Mamma, lean on me," the child told her.
"I will hold you up."

"Otter Boy, I think I have been here before,"
Stone Girl said. "This creek with the boats tied up
I have seen and the tall log house ahead. There was
also a hill peaked like a sugar loaf. I don't see it
now." After passing the woods, the peaked hill came
into view.

The priest had put on his robe. Now he marched
ahead with its skirt flapping. He questioned an old
woman they met, and led his charges on. Behind the
great log house stood stables with wagons and carts
in the wide stable yard. Men came out of the stables
to watch the strange sight of a black-robed priest
with a girl and a small dark Indian boy coming
after. Père Le Clercq was all force and dignity now.
He led them up on the wide veranda and into the
tavern room where players sat at cards. A heavy-
faced man with long red hair behind the bar said Captain Stanton was out at one of his farms but would be
back this evening. The priest took his charges
through a dining room with white cloths on heavy
oak tables and into a parlor on the other side of the
hall. A servant woman with blue calico tied around

her head came to protest that this was the private living quarters of the family. The priest brushed her aside.

"We belong to the family," he said mysteriously in his strange English accent. "Captain Stanton will be glad enough to see us here when he comes."

It was a very fine room, élégant, the priest called it in French, the tongue he always used to Stone Girl. It was in truth more élégant than the petit salon of Madame Corbusier, but it was the curious smell in here that affected the girl most. Sitting here she could close her eyes and feel red clouds again swirl about her. When she opened her eyes, a tall white lamp painted with blue forget-me-nots rose from a table. There were fine chairs and a canapé. A small gold chair stood at the small desk with legs curved like those of a deer. Above it hung a painting of the lady with yellow hair.

Otter Boy kept stirring uneasily.

"Guka, Mamma. Why does the white woman on the wall watch me all the time?" he whispered. "When I came in the door I saw her watch me. Now she watches me over here. I am afraid of white people who watch me."

"Otter Boy. It is nothing to be afraid of. She watches you because her blood is in you. She is

Ohum, your grandmother. Soon she will come in to see you."

"What will she do?" Otter Boy asked uneasily.

"She will look at you with love like Simone's Guka, mamma," Stone Girl promised.

Otter Boy nodded. He seemed satisfied now and kept his eyes on the door but no lady came, only a small girl who gazed at them with hostility. She stuck out her tongue at Otter Boy and vanished. Finally the servant with blue calico on her head came to the door and announced that Captain Stanton was coming. Looking out of the window, they saw nothing but heard a horse and presently a firm step in the hall. Then a man stood in the doorway, not a small pleasant eager little man with red cheeks like Simone's father but a big man like the Yengwe major at Madame Corbusier's, an imposing figure in light breeches and with a dark face that didn't welcome their presence in this room.

The priest rose to his feet but Stone Girl sat very still. Never had she felt such a faintness inside of her.

"I am Father Le Clercq. I have come a long way to see you," the priest announced. "From across the great lake you call Michigan. From Fort Detroit, which once was ours but now belongs to you English."

The assemblyman inclined his head but remained silent. Stone Girl noticed he did not pay reverence to the priest as was customary among those who came to Madame Corbusier's. Père Le Clercq went on.

"I have made this long journey on your behalf, monsieur," he declared, and when the Englishman still said nothing, "I understand that you lost a daughter to the Indians?"

"That is true." A shadow crossed the dark face. "She was stolen from us on the way up from her grandmother's, where her uncle and aunt had taken her. They were both killed and scalped and the boat-men as well."

"You may be thankful that your child was not killed likewise," the priest declared. "What would you have to say if I told you now I had brought your daughter back safe and sound to your bosom?"

The assemblyman looked unmoved.

"I would say it was impossible."

"Nothing is impossible to God," the priest asserted. "As God's servant and advocate, I can tell you now that He looked after your child all these years, protected and sustained her, and now through the efforts of my society she is returned to you. This is she who was dead and is alive again, who was lost and is found."

The assemblyman gave no sign of pleasure, only stared at the priest, then coldly at Stone Girl.

"My daughter has already been returned to me," he announced.

Père Le Clercq was taken aback.

"You are joking, monsieur. Surely you cannot be serious."

"Quite serious. I received my daughter back more than a year ago. She is with me now."

"But are you sure, monsieur?" the priest stammered.

"I am quite sure. She remembered me and living here as a small child. Also she bears a strong resemblance to my wife. The same coloring and hair." He turned to indicate Stone Girl. "On the other hand, this girl whom you claim to be my daughter bears no resemblance to my wife at all."

"I cannot believe it," the priest repeated. He saw the sum of his long arduous journey crumbling. He turned to Stone Girl. "What do you say to this?"

Stone Girl sat with impassive face but inside she had turned to ice.

"The girl who says the lady on the painting is her mother, is she here?" she asked.

"You want to see her?" the assemblyman asked with a kind of indulgence. "She is busy getting ready for her marriage next month to a gentleman from Philadelphia. But I suppose she can come down for a few moments." He left the room. "She'll be here in a little while," he said on his return.

Stone Girl waited. Then the ice in her turned to fever as she looked up and saw two figures in the doorway. One was the child who had stared at them with angry eyes before, the other a slender young lady in a graceful silk dress and with hair like willow twigs in early spring. The assemblyman gazed on her with pride.

"This is the Reverend Le Clercq," he introduced. "And this is a young woman he brought from the Indians thinking she might be you." He smiled faintly.

The young lady bowed to the priest but to Stone Girl and Otter Boy gave no greeting, only a measured look. Now why, Stone Girl asked herself, should the girl's cool secure eyes fetch up in her such a feeling of hatred? She found herself speaking harshly to her in Delaware but no sign of understanding crossed Mary Stanton's face save a kind of contempt at the sound of the guttural speech.

Her father turned sharply to the priest, who questioned Stone Girl in French, then explained in English.

"Claire asked your daughter in Delaware what Indian village she lived in."

"Mary doesn't speak Delaware," her father said at once. "She was captured and adopted by the Shawanees."

"Shawanose understand Delaware," Stone Girl said swiftly. "Not the same but can talk together."

"Well, fortunately," the assemblyman explained to the priest, "Mary was taken from the Shawanees when she was still too young to remember much of anything. A Captain Karricher rescued her at the risk of his own life and she lived with the Karrichers in the Conocheague. Not till General Bouquet brought the captives to Carlisle did Mrs. Karricher hear that we were looking for our daughter. She hated to give her up but the following year brought her here and told us many true things about us that Mary had said. I saw the resemblance to my wife at once and Mary herself remembered her."

"But she don't remember Shawano?" Stone Girl said.

The assemblyman ignored her.

"I have already informed you," he reminded the priest, "how short a time Mary was with the savages. For this I am thankful. Mrs. Karricher, who is my housekeeper now, is a cultivated Christian woman and brought her up as her own daughter, not as an Indian. You yourself can see the result." He indicated the two young women as if to point out the disparity between them. "That's all, Mary. Thank you for coming down." He turned to the priest. "I hope you are satisfied."

"It is a great disappointment, monsieur," Père Le Clercq confessed. He looked at Stone Girl accusingly. "Why did you tell Madame Corbusier and Major Scott these things?"

"I don't tell I look like my mother," she testified. "I am dark. Never Laugh tell me I look like my father."

"Who is this Never Laugh? An Indian?" the assemblyman inquired.

"I don't know her Yengwe name. She is a prisoner like me. She tell me my father's name."

"And how did she say she knew that?"

"She don't say," Stone Girl said.

"Where is this Never Laugh now?"

"She is in the ground."

"So?" The assemblyman turned to the priest grimly. "I'm sorry but this girl is an impostor."

Stone Girl sat uncomprehendingly.

"Père Le Clercq. I am not taught that word. You must tell what it means."

"It means," said the priest, "that you are a fraud and pretender, that you have deceived us."

"I don't deceive," Stone Girl told him stolidly. She pointed to the painting on the wall. "Never Laugh tell me never forget my mother is a lady. I see this lady in my mind."

The assemblyman faced the priest.

"It's a made-up story," he said sternly. "Either the girl did it or, of course, the woman she calls Never Laugh could have planted the whole business in her mind. What else did she tell you, girl?"

"She tell me the lady with yellow hair will run to kiss me when I come," Stone Girl testified. "She says the lady will know me. Maybe you ask her now to come and see if she knows me."

The priest turned to the assemblyman.

"My wife is dead," he said harshly. "She died three months before our daughter was returned."

Stone Girl gave a little nameless native cry.

"Ai! Ekih! She is no more. She is gone and I can never see her again!"

The assemblyman was staring at her.

"The girl is not white. She's Indian," he said with distaste. Turning suddenly, he found watchers and listeners in the doorway, among them the woman in blue calico and the barman with long hair. "What are you doing here?" he demanded angrily, and they vanished.

The priest remained uncomfortable in his chair.

"This puts me in a very difficult position, monsieur," he confessed. "I ransomed the girl from the Wyandots. Madame Corbusier in Fort Detroit paid me what I had paid. Now she expects you to reimburse me so I can reimburse her. There is also the expense of the long journey. I am only a poor servant of the Lord and beg you to find a way for Madame Corbusier to be repaid."

"You can't hold me responsible for your mistakes, Reverend," Captain Stanton told him.

"The girl is a very good worker," the priest persisted. "Madame Corbusier trained her in her own kitchen. She's skilled in French cuisine. I am sure she would be valuable to you as a servant in your inn."

Captain Stanton's face remained cool.

"It's not easy for me to see her working here."

"I could bind her to you for whatever time you say would pay her debt," the priest went on eagerly.

"And if she runs away?"

"Not Claire," he promised. "She has never run away."

Captain Stanton hesitated. He indicated Otter Boy.

"And this child, who is he?"

"It's her child with an Indian father," the priest explained virtuously. "They were duly man and wife in the Indian custom. He is an unusually good child, monsieur, very quiet, and duly baptized in our Christian tradition. He made no trouble either for Madame Corbusier or for me on the way down. He's another reason why as your property she will never run away."

The assemblyman continued to regard the boy with distaste.

"Indians are far from popular around here," he said. "Besides, I could pay you nothing in advance—not until I see how she works out." He considered. "On the other hand, it's true that I can use another girl in the kitchen if you want me to try her."

"You will give her a bed in the inn to sleep in and look after her?" the priest asked. "Madame Corbusier treated her with much kindness."

"She will be treated with due merit." The Captain raised his voice. "Mrs. Karricher!" After a moment a blond woman in a dress with glittering black buttons appeared. "Mrs. Karricher, I have a girl here to help out in the kitchen. She has both cooked and waited on table. You will see that she and the boy have a place to sleep on the third floor."

The woman gazed on Stone Girl and Otter Boy with ill-concealed aversion. From that and something in her pale-blue eyes the girl had the feeling that the woman had overheard the talk in here or had been told by others who had heard it.

It was a rainy evening in June and Captain Peter Stanton sat alone in his private business room. He would have another pipeful before going to bed. The roof dripped audibly on the ground outside, not heavily, just enough to indicate a gentle downpour. None would run off. All would go into the ground. He had seldom seen a more hopeful spring and early summer. Sun and rain this year had come aplenty. Hay would be heavy. Already wheat stood

84

stout throughout the cleared land of the valley. Rye
would be high as a man's head. Not a stalk had been
knocked down by showers. Already corn flourished
and potatoes would soon be in flower.

Oh, the valley could expect bumper crops and
today he would feel gratified had he not done what
he had. It was, you might say, a blunder of the heart
but it remained a blunder. It was true that every
man was entitled to make a mistake once in a while
and he had fallen into this mostly to oblige one of
the clergy. But he should have stood hard and firm
and refused to involve himself with a fraudulent
girl who claimed to be of his own blood, particularly
when she was the mother of an Indian child. Both
were undoubtedly Indians and Indians were not in
favor here these days of savage outrages. Twice the
last month news had come down the river from re-
mote valleys where settlers and their families had
been killed and scalped, their buildings burned and
crops destroyed. No one around here complained
directly to him about the girl. But he saw them
scowl at the Indian boy, and Mrs. Karricher reported that she and others had become uneasy. They
didn't like the presence of a savage among them.
The girl had lied about being his missing daughter
and nothing she said could be believed after that.

For all they knew, she could be in league with the Indians and reporting to them when to strike.

Mrs. Karricher said it would be wisest to bundle the girl and her child off at once, but the Captain didn't like that. He would rather wait for a suitable excuse to discharge her. He had duly signed papers of his own making that so long as the girl remained and was industrious he would employ her and at the end of her service pay a lump sum to this French woman at Fort Detroit. In good time he would find justification to dismiss her but Mrs. Karricher couldn't wait. She promised him a way to get rid of her before that. Oh, she wouldn't pick an outright quarrel with her or she might wake up some night without hair. No, she had other means to convince an undesirable girl of the wisdom of taking French leave.

Captain Stanton didn't know that he liked those means when he heard about them. On the other hand, he comforted himself that they might be the least painful solution for all parties concerned. He looked forward to their consummation. On several occasions Mrs. Karricher convinced him that his Indian maid and her brat would surely disappear during the night, but mornings they were still there, further evidence, if any more were needed, of the girl's Indian blood, for it was well known how a savage could outwait a white man. The assemblyman didn't like the situation. He was glad for Mary's approaching marriage to occupy his mind, and for the fact that his mother planned to attend. Thaddeus Potter, the bridegroom, was bringing her along from Philadelphia and the son had in mind certain ways by which she might be of help to him.

He welcomed the news that the boat with his mother had been sighted. He notified Mary and his younger daughter, Nan. Then he put on a clean ruffled shirt, and all repaired to the riverbank. The water was high from the many rains, the current strong, and the polers had a hard time of it. Nan waited impatiently on one side of him while Mary stood with composure on the other, now and then fluttering a handkerchief to the approaching boat with the mild but personable young lawyer related to the Allens and sure to be favored by the Penns. Peter Stanton didn't know as he looked with much favor on the young man's small clothes and shoes with silver buckles. Bridegroom or no bridegroom, such trappings looked out of place here on the frontier. Just the same, there was a certain satisfaction for a rough citizen on the border to stand here between his two daughters and bask for a while in their rustling dresses and feminine chatter. It brought back to him fleeting memories of their mother in silk mitts and bonnet with the soft perfume of lavender about her and her gentlewoman's voice in his ear.

The family reunion on the riverbank was watched by smiling boatmen and attendants from the inn who had come to help with traveling boxes and other plunder. Peter Stanton's mother held up her wrinkled face to be kissed and told of her trip in Quaker accents that sounded singular here in the back-country depths of the province.

"I feel perfectly normal," she insisted at the inn, having her boxes brought to her so she could give Mary her wedding gift, a silver set designed and engraved by the celebrated Quaker Matthew Downs. She had a present for Nan, too, and a new leather-bound account book for her son. All through dinner she acquainted them with civilizing news from the lower Delaware and Schuylkill rivers as well as the latest brought by ships from the motherland. Not till evening when Nan was in bed and the lovers in the parlor did her son have the opportunity to speak alone with her in her room.

"I must tell you something before you have it from Nan or Mary," he told her.

His mother heard him through in silence.

"Thou meanst this Indian girl claims to be my own granddaughter, Peter?"

"Claimed. Not any more," he corrected.

"But she's still here? Wilt let me see her?"

"You have already seen her," he said, and when she demanded where, "At dinner. She waited on us at the table tonight."

His mother drew back.

"Didst have to make this girl a servant, Peter?"

"The priest begged me to. He brought her a long way and still had a long way to go."

"Thou shouldst have thought of the embarrassment and awkwardness of having her in thy house," she reminded.

"She doesn't stay in the house, Mother. She's in the stable."

"The stable?" his mother repeated slowly. "Dost keep a girl who claims to be thy daughter and a child she says is thy grandson out with the horses?"

His dark weathered face stained.

"I gave her a place in the inn to sleep the first few nights. The priest asked me to. But he didn't understand the temper of our people. You know this isn't the city of Philadelphia, where savages are pampered and justified in every crime they com-

mit on the frontier. This is the frontier itself. Mrs.
Karricher told me my guests didn't feel safe or
complimented sleeping in the same house as Indians.
She said she herself never knew if she'd wake up
alive in the morning. She was especially concerned
over Mary. She reminded me that this Indian girl
we knew nothing about claimed herself to be Mary
and would resent her."

"But how dost thou know she is surely Indian,
Son? I have seen Indians on the street in Philadelphia, where as you know they come to see the
proprietaries. I didn't get the impression that an
Indian girl waited on us at the table tonight."

"She doesn't have to wear leggings and a match-
coat to be a squaw, Mother. I've kept her in calico
so as not to make the guests uneasy. She's very dark,
if you noticed."

"Thou art dark thyself, Peter."

He flushed.

"Perhaps, but I don't go around silent and sullen.
And I don't speak fluent Indian and broken English."

"Dost not suppose, Peter, thou'd be fluent enough
in the Indian tongue if thou'd'st been raised by
Indians? As for English, I had a hard enough time
making thee speak it correctly as a child and there

is no drop of Indian blood in thee so far as I know, although I've often wondered whence came thy wild and militant ways."

He made a wry face.

"At least, Mother, I have no Indian child."

"Not so far as we know, thank Providence," she said.

"And no daughter with a primitive mind, Mother. Now this Indian girl sneaks off from her work to go and sit like a statue by Harriet's grave. At the same time she's completely mystified by Harriet's painting. She probably thinks it's alive. She's been caught several times staring at it in the parlor, where she has no occasion to be. We haven't found anything missing as yet but Mrs. Karricher questioned her as to what she was doing in there. What do you suppose she said? She said she came in to be with what she calls the Tschipey, or ghost. She thinks the painting of Harriet is a ghost."

"Perhaps, although not of necessity," his mother said thoughtfully. "But go on. What else makes thee so certain she's a savage?"

"All her notions are so typically Indian. She told Nan she heard that long ago the white people painted their servants black so they could tell them from their white masters and this went on so long that now slaves are born black. I think she said her Indian grandfather had told her."

"Thou canst not think she believes it literally?" his mother said. "It's only an Indian allegory with elements of truth."

"Of course she believes it. Not only her thinking but her reactions are Indian. Look, Mother. When we first came here there were still two Indians left on the island. We couldn't pronounce their names so we called one Big Fool and the other Little Fool. You'd think they'd resent it. But, no. If you asked them their names, that's what they told you, Big Fool and Little Fool. They didn't seem to mind. Now this girl takes insults the same way. For some reason Nan took a violent dislike to her from the beginning. Mary ignores her, goes her own way as if Claire wasn't there. But Nan goes out of her way to be unpleasant and say sarcastic things especially when I'm not around. You know how difficult Nan can be. Claire takes it all, doesn't seem to mind."

"Dost mean tolerance isn't a virtue?"

"Not when it's shown by Indians. Beware of it then. Indians are trained from childhood to conceal their true feelings till the chance comes to strike. Then they take their revenge."

"Exactly what did Nan say to her, Son?"

"Well, Mrs. Karricher, who knows Indians, told Nan that Indians never married, that they just lived together. Naturally with Mary's wedding coming on, Nan was shocked. She demanded of Claire if she was married. Claire said yes. Who came to your marriage? Nan asked. Nobody comes when an Indian is married, Claire said. Then how were you married? Didn't you have a wedding? Nan asked. That's where Claire's mentality came out. She told Nan that Indians didn't need a wedding like white people. She said a white wife knows her husband is bound to her by law. She can be lazy or mean or fight with him as much as she likes, and he can't do anything about it. And her husband, the same. That's why, Claire said, the white people have a wedding with gifts to bribe the bride and rum to make everybody forget the troubles the couple is going to have. Now the Indian doesn't have to deceive himself, Claire said. His wife isn't bound to him by law. He knows he must be good to her or she will leave him and take his children along. And the Indian wife knows the same about him. So they don't need wedding presents and rum to forget what's going to happen. And they don't need a preacher, Claire said, with a black book to read the lie that

now they will always live happy together. No, Claire
said, the Indian husband and squaw just stay good
to each other and live happy together. Did you ever
hear such nonsense?"

"I must admit there's some truth as well as poetry
in what she says about us," his mother confessed.

"Truth? Well, of course, Mother. Husbands and
wives naturally have their bad moments. I've even
known one or two who didn't speak to each other for
weeks or perhaps months. But that doesn't mean we
have weddings to forget or are to be criticized by
savages who have no civilized ways at all."

"What else did Nan say to this girl, Son?"

"Oh, many things. I believe one time she called
Claire a dirty squaw or something like that. Another
time she told her that Indians lied and couldn't be
trusted. She accused Claire of claiming to be her
sister only to get the money Mary's mother left to
her on her twentieth birthday. She's also made unpleasant remarks about Claire's Indian boy, whom
Nan seems to dislike even more than she does Claire.
Oh, I don't condone it, Mother. I would have
stopped it had I heard about it in time. I suspect
the servants encourage it. Not that it takes too much
encouragement. You know how willful and sharp-
tongued a child without a mother here on the frontier can be."

His mother made a grave face.

"I had hoped," she said, "that Mary's return would be a good influence on Nan's disposition and temper."

"Oh, she has been, she has been," Peter Stanton assured. "A very good influence. It's the presence of this Indian girl claiming to be her sister that has upset and outraged the child. We must get rid of her, Mother, and I'm counting on you to accomplish it."

"What hast thou done about it thyself, Son?" his mother asked.

"There's little I can do short of discharging her," he confessed unhappily. "And I don't want to anger her. She might take revenge on Nan sometime or on me by burning down the inn or the stables. Mrs. Karricher's husband was an Indian fighter and she agrees it's wisest to persuade her to leave on her own volition. To that end she and the girls in the kitchen have been making it unpleasant for her. They've given her what they call the silent treatment. They decline to have anything to do with her. They put salt in her tea and red pepper in her and the boy's food. Several times Mrs. Karricher felt the girl was on the point of leaving, but an Indian's skin is thick. It seems they can wait forever and the two of them are still here."

His mother gazed steadily into his eyes.

"Why dost thou suppose she stays?"

"Who knows? There's no probing the Indian mind. Her life here is probably better than with her own people. Then I wonder sometimes if it could be for Nan. The girl seems to have taken a fancy to her, perhaps because Nan is white and very fair while her own child is Indian and very dark. Mrs. Karricher says she's caught the girl looking at Nan with a kind of worship despite the bad times Nan gives her."

"Hast thou never seen Mrs. Karricher looking at Mary with a kind of worship?" his mother inquired.

"Why do you ask that?" Peter Stanton came back sharply. "Mrs. Karricher has every right to, Mother. It's perfectly natural for her. She raised Mary as her own child before bringing her to me. But this Indian girl's worship of Nan is purely primitive, the blind admiration of a savage for a white child."

"Dost thou think so?" the old lady said.

"What else could it be?" he demanded. "It's unaccountable and unnatural any other way. In any event, it may be our salvation. I thought perhaps, Mother, when you went back to Philadelphia you might take Nan with you for a visit as you did Mary when she was a child. Once Nan's gone, we have a notion our dusky Indian maiden will take her own child and fade into the forest and that's the last we'll see of her."

Mrs. Stanton's face had sobered.

"I must think it over, Son," she said. "It was nearly fifteen years ago when Mary visited me. I am older now and thou'st just admitted that thy child does not make the sweetest of companions."

◆ *ix* ◆

FOR some time sleep had not come easily to Stone Girl. It must be the strange sleeping place, she told herself, or the bed she lay on. The beds in Madame Corbusier's house had been young and strong. This bed was old and very weak. Many people had lain on it. The cover had long since been worn through, so that the corn husks pushed out like the insides of a gutted deer. Also, it was a narrow bed. She and Otter Boy had to lie very close or one would fall off.

It was not a flat bed. At the place for their heads, the bed rose up like a boulder. She thought she knew now why white people seldom stood straight as Indians. They had slept on such a bed and it had bent them like ice bends the young birch trees.

Beneath her she could hear the horses stamp. They sneezed from the hay dust and pulled on their mangers with their strong teeth. The couch and blanket smelled rank of them. Once during the night, when a rat ran over their legs, Otter Boy whispered.

"Guka, Mamma, why do you shake? Is it the rat?"

"No, it is not the rat."

"Is it the cold of the night?"

"Otter Boy, it is not the cold. Our uncle, Sisquanachan, the south wind, is with us."

"Guka, Mamma, is it Kamlus, the sickness that shakes again and again?"

"Otter Boy. Go into sleep. It is not Kamlus, the sickness that shakes again and again."

"Guka, Mamma, do you know the old dried-up white woman who came yesterday? The one that looks like she will not breathe very long."

"I do not know her. I only wait on her at the table."

"Guka, Mamma, she stopped by the stable today

when you were in the kitchen. She asked my name. Was it weak or brave that I told her?"

"It is right that you tell her when she asks."

"She did not say go away or be quiet. She talked like she knew me. Does she know me, Guka, Mamma?"

"Otter Boy. Perhaps she knows you. She is Ohum, the grandmother of your Guka, mamma. But you must never tell her that. She would not believe. She would be angry."

"Why must I never tell her?"

Stone Girl lay silent a while.

"Otter Boy. It is because she is a white person. Surely you have seen by this time how unaccountable white persons are. Sometimes when the morning is bad and stormy, they will say good morning, and sometimes when the morning is very good and the sun smiles, they will say nothing. You have heard them call you Johnny or Indian Charley or something else that is not your name. An old man of the Chippeways told me once the white man does this because inside of him he feels guilty and afraid. He knows he is a trespasser on Indian land and that Indians fight and kill those who steal their land. So he calls you Indian Johnny to make you seem little and harmless and himself big and victorious. He is

like Andahammie, the great green bullfrog, who bel-
lows fearfully at you like Gisilija, the wild bull, but
dives in the mud to hide himself when you come by."

"Guka, Mamma, why doesn't the white man want
a brave Indian like me in the house?"

"Otter Boy. You are little and would get into
mischief."

"There is a little girl in the house and she can get
into mischief, too."

"She belongs to the house. She is not Indian."

"Guka, Mamma, why does the white man think he
is better than the Indian?"

"Ehih! Otter Boy. That is a puzzle. Your great-
grandfather, Machilek, said it was because the white
man has talking books and the talking books tell
him he is better than other men. The Indian does
not need talking books to lie like the bird who sings
a sweet story and then flies away. From the time he
is little the Indian's father and grandfather teach
him the truth that all men and beasts and living
things are brothers and cousins and must be treated
with respect."

"Guka, Mamma. But the white men on the boat
had no talking books and they thought themselves
better than us."

"Otter Boy. There is more than one reason. I

heard your father, Espan, once say that the white
man thinks himself better because he alone knows
how to make a gun. If the Indian needs a gun, he
must pay the white man many furs. If he has no
furs, he must take his bow and arrow and tramp a
whole winter in the forest. His feet must go silent
like Long Tail, the panther. He must always go
into the wind. He must crawl like a snake to get
close enough for his arrows. Now the white man
with a gun need not do this. His gun kills the deer
a long way off. In war he even has a bigger gun he
calls a cannon that kills more than one man with a
single shot. All this makes the white man's nose very
high and proud."

"Guka, Mamma. But the woman with black buttons doesn't have a gun. And she is the proudest
of all."

"Otter Boy. There is still another reason. It is
the Yengwe's pale skin. Your grandfather, Feast
Maker, told me the pale skin comes from being
afraid. You yourself know how fearful the white
man is of poor Pitquok, the moth. He is still more
afraid of other white men. He hangs heavy oaken
doors on his houses and hides his ornaments in an
iron box. But most of all he is fearful of dirt and
scrubs every speck of dirt from his skin. He has

done this so many years that today his skin is white
and thin. Now the Indian is not a fearful man. He
hangs only a loose hide for a door to his cabin.
When he goes away, he just lays a stick across on
the ground outside and no Indian would think of
going in or taking anything. Least of all is he fearful of dirt. He knows that his mother, the Earth, is
of dirt and heals him. He sees corn and beans and
nuts and pawpaws and sweet tobacco all come out
of the dirt. So he has never scrubbed the good earth
color from his skin."

"Guka, Mamma. I always thought the white man
looked sick. Now I know he is only pale from scrubbing and fear," Otter Boy said. "Guka, Mamma.
If you don't shake now, perhaps I can go to sleep."

The next afternoon was Sunday, when the inn
served cold meats and breads for supper. Stone Girl
had an hour free with Otter Boy in their room. All
week the sun had been hot on the stable roof and the
door of the room stood open for stable air. It was
almost time to go back to her work when she heard
voices first below and then on the creaking stable
stairs. Otter Boy, who ran to the door, came back
with a startled face. Soon someone knocked politely
on the open door.

"May I come in?" a voice asked, and it was Ohum,

the grandmother. Her son, Captain Stanton, loomed tall and dark-faced behind her.

Stone Girl stood up as she had been taught in front of her elders. She had also been taught to welcome the guest with food and drink and a place to sit down, but of these she had none. So she just stood while the grandmother gave a sickening look around the room, then at the girl with dismay.

"It is very warm," the visitor made talk. "I am told thou speakest the Delaware language. How dost say it is warm in Delaware?"

"We say Wusca or Ktschingiehellen, it has much sunshine."

The lady repeated the words with difficulty. All of them except Captain Stanton had to smile.

"It must be a very hard language for thee to learn," she said.

"Not hard for an Indian."

"But I believe thou saidst thou'rt white?" the grandmother questioned, glancing at her son for confirmation.

Stone Girl froze. Her smile had vanished.

"I am Indian," she said. "Indian language come easy for me."

"But when thou first camest didst not thou tell my son thou'rt white and had been taken by the In-

dians when very young? Didst even claim to be
Mary, my son's daughter?"

The brown girl stood very rigid.

"I say what Never Laugh tell me. Captain Stanton say is a big lie. White woman Karricher say is a
big lie. Girl Mary say is big lie. Captain Stanton
say I am Indian. White woman Karricher say I am
Indian. Girl Mary say I am Indian. All but Never
Laugh say I am Indian."

Captain Stanton heard her with satisfaction.

"You see, Mother, it's as I told you? She doesn't
even believe this invention herself."

"She didn't say that," his mother declared, and
turned to the girl. "Didst mean, Claire, thou wast
raised Indian but art really white?"

"I am Indian," she maintained.

"Claire, tell me about the painting on the wall of
the inn," the grandmother persisted. "Didst not
say thou hadst seen the woman in the painting before? Didst not recognize the woman as thy
mother?"

At the mention of the painting, Stone Girl kept
her face with difficulty.

"Is true I see painting on the wall when I come.
She is beautiful white lady with yellow hair. Never
Laugh say my mother is beautiful white lady with

yellow hair. But my father, Feast Maker, say my mother is Clanpeechan, Still Water. She have black hair and is Indian. My grandfather, Machilek, say my mother is Indian. Captain Stanton say my mother is Indian. All say my mother is Indian."

The old lady looked baffled.

"But I understand that thou thyself claimst to remember other things including my brick house?"

"What is brick house?" the girl asked stolidly. "I see stone house in dream. Stone is red. Everything in dream is red. Sky is red. Cloud is red. All is red. What is brick house? I do not know brick house."

Captain Stanton took his mother's arm.

"I think we've had enough of this, Mother. I hope you're satisfied. I told you how it would be but you wouldn't believe me."

His mother refused to give up so easily.

"Peter, wouldst leave me alone with Claire for a while? I appreciate thy bringing me up. Now I think I can find my way down or Claire can show me."

Captain Stanton looked displeased.

"I don't like you to be up here alone," he told her.

"Nonsense," she said. "I'm safe here with Claire and her child as with thee."

You could see that he didn't believe that.

"You must be reasonable, Mother. After I told you about Claire, you kept after me until I agreed to let you speak to her. You knew I didn't like to have the subject opened again. Especially not before Mary's wedding. It's as if I distrust my own daughter and you your own granddaughter. But I finally agreed to let you talk to her. Now you have her answer. I feel the matter has gone far enough."

"I have promised thee, Son, to do nothing to upset Mary's wedding," his mother reminded. "I only wish to speak to Claire in private for a few minutes. Thou didst not wish me to speak to her in thy house and I must return to Philadelphia after the wedding."

Captain Stanton set his mouth. With a stern face he left.

"I'll wait for you downstairs," he said.

When he had gone, the grandmother closed the door and turned to the girl.

"Claire, wilt listen carefully to me? I wish thee to forget my son and everyone else and tell me the truth. Art thou really Mary Stanton who was stolen from us by the Indians?"

Stone Girl's face was cruel to the old woman gazing at her with such appeal.

"I am Stone Girl," she repeated doggedly.

"But thy name was once Mary Stanton, wasn't it?"

"Madame Corbusier in Fort Detroit call me Claire," she answered. "But Stone Girl is my name. My Indian father give it to me."

"But thou wast not Indian originally. Thou wast white, wast not?"

"A child cannot help how he is born," she said stoically. "My father, Feast Maker, don't like white people. He rub white off of me till I am all Indian. See, my eyes are dark. My hair is dark. My skin is dark. I am Indian."

Stone Girl thought the old woman looked at her with compassion and yearning.

"Claire, I am thy friend. Perhaps I am even thy grandmother. Wilt bare thy shoulders and breasts to me so I can see that all the white is rubbed off thee as thou sayst?"

The girl's answer was to turn to Otter Boy, speak to him in Delaware, and have him take off his shirt. Then she spoke to her caller in English.

"See his chest. He is Indian. See his back and shoulders. He is Indian all over. He is my son. I am his mother. My son is Indian. I am Indian, too."

The first bitter expression crossed the old lady's face.

"Thou art just like my son when he was young, Claire, stubborn and determined to be wild and lead his own life in the forest. Why dost thou do this to me?"

Stone Girl did not say anything. The two women stood facing each other for a long time while the boy's black eyes searched one face, then the other. The older gave in first.

"I am a tired old woman, my child. I won't force myself on thee. If thou dost not want me, I shall have to get along without thee as best I can."

Stone Girl did not reply till the older woman was at the door.

"Ohum," she said. "You ask question. One time my grandfather, Machilek, tell me a story. It is long story. It is an Indian story. Maybe you don't want to hear long Indian story?"

"Yes, indeed, I do," the old lady said, turning. "Wilt tell it to me?" she asked courteously, and Stone Girl began.

"One time long while ago, Shipahap, the blue squirrel, live in the forest. All day he leap on the trees. At night he swing in his nest on top of Talala, the white cedar. He never think of himself and who he is till Wuloawa, the black fox, came along. Wulo-awa say to him, Shipahap, you are not really one of us. My father was black and your father was black

but your mother was gray and you are blue. That
is no color for a squirrel. Shipahap listened politely
but say nothing till Woapink, the possum, who is
almost white and knows very much of the world,
came along. Shipahap, he said, I can only hang by
my tail on a branch of the tree but you can fly
happy from one tree to another. You are really a
bird and don't know it. Nunscheach, the she-bear,
come crashing through the woods. What is all this
about? she say. And when she hear, she say, Shipahap, you live high in the trees. You don't belong
with us on the ground. It is very plain you are of the
race that go suspended in air. You are a bluebird,
that's what you are. But I can't sing, Shipahap
said. I only cough and make kissing sounds with
my mouth. That, say Nunscheach, is because you
live too long with squirrels. Now you go to your
own people, the bluebirds. They will show you how
to sing and eat little worms." Stone Girl broke off.
"I tell you it is a long story. It is too long perhaps?"

"No, not at all. Please go on," Ohum, the grandmother, begged her, and Stone Girl continued.

"Well, Shipahap, the squirrel, don't like to eat
little worms. He rather stay where he was and be
squirrel but he always hear that Woapink, the
possum, is very wise, and Nunscheach, the she-bear,

must not be crossed, so he let Nunscheach, the she-bear, and Woapink, the possum, and Wuloawa, the black fox, take him to Schwanacook the horned snake. But Schwanacook say, it is not him who does magic things like make water both fall down from the sky and up from the ground. It is his cousin, Shachamel, the straight fish that white people call the eel. He is very powerful. It is he who tells the sun in the evening when to set and in the morning to rise. So they went to Shachamel, the straight fish, who came up out of the water to watch Shipahap fly in the trees. You are not Shipahap, the squirrel, but Tshimalus, the bluebird, he said, and what are you doing with a long tail? The Great Spirit gave Tshimalus a nice short tail. And what are you doing with four feet and four claws? It is not seemly for a bluebird to have more than two feet and two claws. So Shipahap gave up his long bushy tail and his back feet and claws. Then Wuloawa, the black fox, and Nunscheach, the she-bear, and Woapink, the possum, and Schwanacook, the horned snake, and Shachamel, the straight fish, took him to the bluebirds. Here is your brother, Shipahap, they said, but the bluebirds gave one look at him and took themselves high up in the trees. He is not one of us, they said. And when Shipahap tried to show them how he could fly through the trees, he fell to the ground. He couldn't leap from limb to limb any more without his long bushy tail to guide him and he couldn't catch fast without his back claws to hold him. And now he was neither Tshimalus, the bluebird, or Shipahap, the squirrel, but an outcast like Skaak, the skunk, and must live by himself, for nobody will live with him."

When she finished, Otter Boy's young black eyes were fastened on her but what she felt most conscious of was the tragic pity on the withered face of Ohum, the grandmother, as she came and put her arms around her.

"Oh, my dear, my dear!" she said.

Stone Girl disliked to be felt sorry for but neither did she like to jerk away from Ohum. Long after her visitor had gone she stood there remembering the moment when Ohum, the grandmother, had been so close. She knew now, she told herself, how Simone must have felt with her own white mother's face against her cheek and the sweet smell of mothers rising about her.

$$\blacklozenge \quad x \quad \blacklozenge$$

WHEN Stone Girl woke during the night a faint white light seemed to hang in the stable room, and all the bustle and preparations in the inn next day were almost as if for her own wedding. Hunters brought deer, bear, and turkey from the forest. Half a dozen bloody carcasses hung from gibbets of poles outside. The inn's kitchen simmered with heat and with the wheaten smells of baking bread, cake, and pie. The black-garbed minister came in time for

dinner, was closeted with the bride, and afterward
the words Mary Stanton had picked for her wedding
text were gravely told from mouth to mouth together with strange-sounding name and numerals
where the text could be found in the black book of
the white people. All the talk that flew in the kitchen
now concerned the wedding: the bride and bridegroom, the gold the bride would have from her dead
mother, and her bride's gown, not borrowed like the
usual wedding garment or christening robe, but
brand-new, never worn before. Indeed it had been
cut out and stitched by the fingers of a downriver
woman Mrs. Karricher had brought up for the occasion. Everything seemed propitious. The sun that
morning came up as usual. Rain had fallen during
the night but Lomache, the north wind, had blown
away the clouds, so that the distant mountains rose
like green walls. Seldom had Stone Girl seen a fairer
day. It must be, she told herself, that even Getanitowit had given his blessing to the wedding. The arriv-
ing guests shot off their muskets in celebration as
they approached. The inn filled. The talk and chatter reminded Stone Girl of a concourse of waterfowl
on the swamps of the White Woman's River.

She moved silently at her duties among the festivi-
ties. Not for nothing had she been called Stone Girl.

When Mary Stanton came down the stairs in her satin bride's gown, the dark-faced girl gave one level look, then remained blind to her, doing her chores in a white apron furnished by the inn. The table in the parlor had been covered for the occasion with a cloth and the cloth with bottles and glasses. Here, as directed by Mrs. Karricher, who presided over everything, she handed drinks to the favored guests crowded in the parlor while the red-headed barkeeper served the less fortunate ones in the hall. When all had been fortified, the wedding service began.

Standing motionless at attention to refill glasses wanted during the ceremony, Stone Girl waited, her face unreadable, listening to the curious words and incantations of the white people. She hoped those who stood with her understood them better than she did, but she knew why they needed brandy at the start. It was to support them through the interminable wedding sermon that followed the prayer and reading from the black book. Now Indian people, she reflected, could stand all day patient, never moving a muscle, listening to the spoken word. But white men were restless, inattentive, and unmanageable like children. The enigmatic words of the lesser incantations and the shouting of the sermon she let roll from her ears like water from the back of Kaak, the wild goose. Not till the exhortations were done and the sorceries of the ceremony itself begun did she pay fast attention, and now through the solemn challenges, responses, and declarations her dark eyes kept fastened on the pale face, white skin, and panther hair of the bride. At the end when the black art of the small black book was finished, and the bride kissed and felicitated, Stone Girl attended again, as directed by Mrs. Karricher, to the liquid refreshment of the guests.

Up to now all had seemed fair and auspicious. It was as if Getanitowit had forgotten her and Otter Boy, washed his hands of them both. Perhaps he had been defeated by the god of the black book of the white people, chased westward like his red subjects. Then suddenly during the wedding dinner two men in deerskin shirts and haggard faces came into the midst of the gaiety, asking to see the Captain. At a word from them he took them into his private business room and shut the door. When they came out, he ordered them to be fed. They ate ravenously in the kitchen but would say nothing. The Captain, they said, had sworn them to silence till the wedding night was over. But Stone Girl noticed that certain men guests were taken into the private room and that when they came out they turned strange hard looks on her as they passed while the women to whose sides they returned looked at her with a kind of horror. What had she done now? she wondered.

"The Indian needn't do anything," she answered herself. "He need only be Indian to be wrong."

At the wedding frolic that followed the dinner, a roan-headed settler played a lively fiddle and the black-garbed preacher joined in the dancing. But all through the revelry Stone Girl thought she caught the high shrill note of strain, and when she came among the dancers to serve them they seemed to look at her with mingled hatred and fear. Whatever it was, it had infected the kitchen now, and all evening the help gave her a wider berth than usual, moving noticeably away from her when she was in the room.

Snatches of guarded talk rose to her ears as she passed but not till late in the night when Mrs. Karricher finally dismissed her for the day did she know for certain what had occurred. As she went back to Otter Boy in the darkness, Billy the hostler heard her and came out of his room with his lantern.

"Your friends better not try their tricks around here tonight," he called after her grimly.

Stone Girl had halted on the stable stairs.

"Who are my friends?" she asked.

"Your Injun friends," he said. "Didn't they tell you in the inn? They're burning and massacreeing up the North Branch."

Stone Girl said nothing. She remained stolid under his hard gaze but inside of her a fierce joy rose. So the Great Spirit had not forgotten his red people. He had not been defeated and banished by the god of the white race. He was still powerful, the protector of his chosen ones. He had put iron into the Indian heart to strike back for their stolen homelands, to drive out the invaders of the forest and rivers of the Original People. Then she went up to Otter Boy in his dark room and told him the news.

Already before dawn they heard men's voices in the stable courtyard, and when she and Otter Boy came down at daylight, Captain Stanton was leaving the back door of the inn. His eyes darkened at the sight of her.

"Claire, I want you to keep that Indian boy of yours out of sight," he told her. "Somebody around here may hurt him."

Then he got on his horse and rode away followed by his men, all with rifles, some on horses but most of them on foot.

Stone Girl turned to see Billy the hostler watching them go.

"They're going to help bury the poor souls your
people butchered," he said to her grimly. "I hope
they teach them savages a lesson. Now get up outa
here, boy, like the Captain said and see how you
stay up."

In the days that followed, Otter Boy wasted in his
stable room. His dark red color faded. His one joy
was to hear the news of Indian successes when his
mother came back from the inn in the evening. She
told him the tales the refugees had brought, of the
cabins, barns, and grain patches burned, of flour and
other white belongings scattered through the woods,
of a Yengwe boy taken bringing in his father's
cattle from the woods, of a pale-haired girl gone
back to their abandoned house for something forgotten and never seen again, of bloody clothes
found on the trail to a spring that flowed red from
battle. There were other tales she did not repeat,
such as a baby found in its cradle with the mark of a
tomahawk in its small skull. That was a white man's
lie, she told herself. Indian men had children and
grandchildren of their own at home. They did not
fight babies.

There was much to relate to him. She told what

the refugees themselves claimed had started the
war. Some believed it dissatisfaction over the land
bought last year from the Indians and opened to
settlers. Some said a white man, Stump, was the
cause. He had murdered five peaceful Indians and
burned their bodies in a cabin. The white people
had never punished him for his crime and now the
Indians were taking the matter into their own hands.

Then on Sunday morning came the gravest news
of all. Manasink Valley on the North Branch had
been attacked, the fort taken, and the settlers killed
or driven off. It was the capture of the fort in the
great valley that shook the people in the inn. News
of the savage victory had spread among the Indians
like wildfire, refugees said. All through the wilderness the tribes were rising.

"Won't you stay and help defend us?" the black-
coated preacher asked fleeing men who stopped over-
night at the inn. "Our captain and most of his men
are away."

But none could be held back from the security of
the south. That day and next the indefensible
wooden inn emptied like a basin suddenly riddled
with holes. Those who remained the preacher invited
to the protection of his stone house with a spring in
the cellar. The bride and bridegroom left hurriedly

with their traps on the boat in which the bridegroom had come. Instead of Ohum, Mrs. Karricher
went along.

"Take me with you, Mary!" Nan cried, following
them to the river, but they said there was no room
in the boat. She must wait till her father got back.

Stone Girl had gone after her with some of the
child's belongings. Now she waited while the small
girl watched the boat move farther and farther
downstream. Nan's face worked with disappointment. It convulsed with anger when she turned and
saw Stone Girl standing there.

"What did you have to tag after me for?" she
accused bitterly and ran back to her room.

The grandmother urged gravely that Stone Girl
and Otter Boy come to the protection of the preacher's stone house but the girl said they would stay
where they were. The red-headed barkeeper had
already left down the river on foot. The cook and
other help went their own way while Billy the stable-
man and the deaf-and-dumb youth who helped him
vanished like partridges into the bush. That night
no living thing but Stone Girl and Otter Boy was
left in the stable.

It seemed ghostly to lie awake and, for the first
time since they had come, hear the sound of neither

horses nor men below. The inn next morning when they went over for breakfast was like a tomb. Once or twice they thought they heard shouts but no one appeared. Close to noon a medley of curious sounds rose from the direction of the river.

"Guka, Mamma," Otter Boy said. "Maybe our brothers have come and we are not there to meet them."

When they reached the bank, they stared in surprise. A sight lay before them that had not been seen in the wilderness before. The whole stretch of water a mile wide and several miles up and down stream was alive with fleeing settlers. Flatboats, keelboats, poleboats, hollow-tree canoes, birch- and elm-bark canoes, pine-log rafts, and even hog troughs made up the flotilla. Anything that floated was crowded with cargo. There were women and children, chickens, small pigs, together with piles of traps, plunder, and belongings. At each riffle the women and children jumped out in bare legs and feet to push their particular flotsam through the shallows. On shore in single file keeping abreast of their families marched men and boys, some driving cattle, some with horses and carts, most of them on foot with muskets in their hands. They looked with certain misgivings at Stone Girl and especially

Otter Boy. A gray-bearded settler stopped briefly to ask where they were. He and all the rest had come from the West Branch, he told her, and were lucky to get away with their hair.

"They's nobody left on our farms now," he mourned. "Nobody but Injuns."

The two watchers waited on the bank while the convoy passed. They stood almost motionless till the last straggler had vanished downstream.

"Guka, Mamma," Otter Boy said. "The white man comes. But he goes, too. He scares and runs away. He is not like the brave Indian."

"Now they are gone," Otter Boy said that night when they went to bed. "Tomorrow you can be with me."

But hardly had the first streaks of daylight appeared when unaccustomed sharp sounds rose from the other end of the valley. They came again and again, barking short and quick, sometimes once, sometimes twice, sometimes many close together.

"Guka, Mamma, what do we hear?" Otter Boy asked. "Is it a dog?"

"No, it is not a dog," Stone Girl said.

"Is it thunder?"

"Otter Boy, I think it is not thunder."

Stone Girl got up and Otter Boy followed. When they reached the stable yard they could see black smoke rising in columns down the valley.

"Guka, Mamma. I spoke right. It was thunder. I can see where the forked tongue licked at the trees."

"Otter Boy. It was not the forked tongue, I think, but our Indian brothers who are here."

"Guka, Mamma—"

"Sehe, hush," she told him. "Someone comes and he is not Indian."

From the woods beyond the field they could hear a thrashing. Presently a figure burst out of the brush and trees, a white man with a half-filled sack and nothing more except the clothes on his back. Stone Girl remembered seeing his face several times around the stable but never had he turned on her such a look of hate and terror as he ran on toward the river.

"Guka, Mamma. Why did he look at us like that?" Otter Boy asked.

"It is the white man's look at the Indian," she told him.

"Guka, Mamma. What did our Indian brothers do to him that he ran?"

"There are many things they do," she told him. "It is to rid the white man from their land."

For a time they stood staring at the rising columns of smoke.

"Guka, Mamma. Are our Indian brothers cold? Do they burn the white man's house to get warm?"

"Otter Boy. Our brothers are not cold. They burn the houses and crops so the land can go back to the Indian forest and game."

"Do they burn the stone house of the preacher, too?"

Stone Girl felt a chill.

"Otter Boy. They don't burn the stone house. Only the roof and what is inside."

The boy looked up at her face quickly as if he detected something in her voice.

"Guka, Mamma. Isn't it good our people have come and that we are Kitchi Kitchi, victorious?"

"It is good," she told him.

"Don't the white people deserve to die for all the bad things they have done to us?"

"They have done many bad things," she agreed.

"Guka, Mamma. Aren't you glad the white sister who spits in our faces is scalped and can't say bad things to us any more?"

Stone Girl held herself with difficulty.

"Otter Boy. I think perhaps she will never say bad things to you again."

"Guka, Mamma. Will our Indian brothers come and burn our stable, too, so we have no place to sleep?"

"They will come, I think," his mother answered, and turned away to the inn. The doors were unlocked and she went in. From the parlor wall she took down the painting of the lady with yellow hair, carried it swiftly to the woods, where she hid it in a clump of young hemlock.

"Now it is in the hand of Getanitowit," she told Otter Boy.

It was almost unbearable waiting. The sun rose red over the blackened wheatfields. It seemed odd to hear the crows call this day like always from the edge of the woods. There followed a great silence in the valley. Between watches the girl got the child and herself snatches of breakfast from what food remained. Afterward the pair stood for a while motionless on the road in front of the inn. But no one came. The valley lay like a dead thing, soundless, unstirring. Never before had it slept like this in the daytime. It was like the hush before the thunder. Any moment now, Stone Girl felt, violence must break out. But nothing happened. In the end she set their faces down the road to the stone house by the run where the preacher lived. Only a month ago she had seen the woods around this house white with Taquach, the dogwood, and before that with the pretty white star flowers of Schwanaminek, the shad tree. Now the limestone walls stood blackened and ruined, the roof gone. Faint smoke still rose from within.

Staring at it, Stone Girl remembered the stories in her home village. Old men would sit peacefully smoking in front of their cabins and tell of burning a house like this. It was the wickedness of the white vandal that had brought it on him. He had taken possession of Indian land as if the Great Spirit had given it to him. He had destroyed the trees, cut them down not for winter warmth but to pile and burn in huge wanton fires so that the smoke drove the game away in the forest. Not satisfied, he had turned up even the sacred Indian earth with his ground cutter and crusher. For a while the Indian had endured him, hoping he would get tired and go away. In the end he found the only way to get rid of the white plunderer was to destroy him and the work of his hands. He had lain in the forest watching and hating the white profaner, then early in the morning descended on him! Ehih! What a difference now. He

who had been so bold and shameless begged like a
woman for his life. The Indian teller of tales would
hold his pipe from his mouth and mimic the fearful
faces, the useless prayers to the white man's gods.
The villagers had heard the story many times. They
stood around waiting for the happy ending, that the
white man had paid for his crimes with blood and
scalps and with burned houses and crops for the
burning of the Indian forest.

Today here by the blackened walls of the preacher
there were no tales or mimicry. The story was
flesh. The ruined house gazed mutely out at her
from its sightless sockets. Stone Girl could feel no
hate or happy ending. She went to the open doorway and pushed a pole through the ashes, hunting
for something she didn't find. Otter Boy was staring
at the sprawled figures on the ground.

"Guka, Mamma. Isn't it good for this to happen?
Isn't it good?" he begged her.

Stone Girl did not answer. Her face was cruel as
she hunted among the scattered tools to dig a shallow grave.

"Guka, Mamma. Why do you do that? Does the
white Ohum feel when she is dead?"

"No, but you and I do so," she told him. "Perhaps
someday you will put a blanket over the face of your

Guka, mamma, to keep it from the stones and ground of the grave."

The boy strained against his mother, pulling at her skirt.

"Guka, Mamma. Let us talk of other things. Let us talk of the white sister who spits in our faces. Where is she?"

"Otter Boy. We will look farther," Stone Girl told him, and led the way to other small farms in the forest. Here the buildings had been of logs and were ashes now. There were few bodies and no Nan. Most of these people had fled down the river. At the last house in the valley embers still glowed. Stone Girl said they would wait for them to cool off to get close enough to search the ashes.

"Guka, Mamma. I do not like this place," Otter Boy whispered. "I see a green bush walking."

Stone Girl turned. From the edge of the woods a bush moved silently and insidiously toward them across the stumpy field.

"Otter Boy. It looks like a bush but it is a man. I think it is one of our people."

She did not say more. Sight of the walking bush had taken her back again to the home village. How often had she seen young Indian boys play war with small green bushes uprooted from the forest in front of them. They played on the knoll in the center of the barked cabins. It was here that girls played, too, trying to hold their balance on a sled of slippery elm bark. She could see in her mind the alder marshes around the village, and hear the sound of a loving Indian father patiently teaching his infant son Al-lamuin, the war whoop. It was here she had first been aware that Espan had taken notice of her.

She waited until the green bush was halfway across the blackened flax patch.

"Nimat, brother," she called in the Delaware tongue. "Why do you hide your face to your own people?"

The bush stopped stock-still. After a moment a voice in the same tongue answered from behind it.

"Auween lacke? Who are you?"

"I am Lenape. And this is my Lenape son."

The bush moved a little closer.

"Ta koom? Where do you come from?"

"I come from the town by the deer lick near the White Woman's branch of the Muskingum, if you know where that is."

"Kih. I know where the Muskingum flows better than a woman," the voice rebuked her. The bush was thrown aside, disclosing a painted face and curly maple rifle behind it, a face young as or

younger than hers and scornful of a girl. The two
gazed at each other and she guessed instantly that
under the paint he was not Indian born. He went
on imperiously. "What do you do here? I watched
you from the time you came from the house of the
horses this morning. When do the white captain
and his soldiers come out of the big house to fight?"

So that, Stone Girl thought, was why the inn
had not been attacked and burned. The youth had
been sent to keep watch on it and report while his
brothers retreated with their booty.

"I look for the Tschipey, ghost, of the small
white girl with yellow hair."

"What is she to you?"

"I am born Yengwe like you," Stone Girl told
him. "She is the small white sister."

He stared at her a long time but what went on
in his mind, whether his thoughts were Indian or
white, there was no telling.

"The small girl with yellow hair is not your white
sister." Then he said bluntly. "She is Indian."

Now why, Stone Girl asked herself, should that
dismay her? All morning she had doggedly faced
the grim prospect of Nan's death. But now that she
was alive, alarm seized her at the fate of the child
and what ordeal lay ahead. She reminded herself
that she, Stone Girl, had lived through it, the stern

captors, the forced marches, the strange, sometimes revolting food, the cold nights on the ground, the sight of forbidding alien faces around her, and the sound of their unintelligible tongue in her ear. But how would it be with the small, weak sister?

"Nimat. You will take me to your brothers?" she asked him.

"You are a woman," he told her coldly. "I cannot do so."

"Nimat, brother. If you tell me the meeting place, it will be enough."

"Woman. The meeting place is where it can't be found. It is hidden by the creek and the mountainside. It is too far for a young woman and a small boy."

"It is not too far for squaws with children to make pilgrimage from the Tuscarawas to the graves of their fathers on the Susquehanna," she reminded him. "It is a long way from Fort Detroit on the Great Sweet Water but I am here."

"The small sister cries too much," he said harshly. "I think by this time she does not breathe."

The face of Never Laugh rose before Stone Girl's eyes and the pale scraps of soft hair she had stroked and mourned over.

"You have told me enough. We will find," she said.

He looked at her uneasily.

"I have told you nothing. I am only Wtegowa, a follower, a recruit, with these men from the country of the Twightwees. My own village on the Tuscarawas I am banished from. How could I tell you anything?"

"Alla leni. It is true," Stone Girl assured him. "You have said nothing. I don't know you. Never have I seen you. I have forgotten you already."

He gave her a strange look, a look of surprise and something almost respect, a look she remembered seeing more than once on Espan's face when she defied him. Now he glanced up at the sun, turned, and without speaking more struck down the valley path that stretched away at the edge of the forest.

✦ *xii* ✦

STONE GIRL stood watching him before taking after. He was soon among the trees and out of sight but the path was an ancient one, trod deeply into the forest mold and broad enough for two men to tramp side by side. Once when another path broke away to the north she caught a glimpse of him far ahead at the next turn as if he had lingered to make sure she took the right fork. Then he was gone but it left the feeling of a faint bond between them. He allowed no further glimpse of himself. The path penetrated more deeply into the forest. It ran in bright-green stretches of hardwoods where the way lay very plain and through stands of ancient pines and hemlocks where it seemed that night was falling and the footway vanished into a floor of smooth brown needles. Only slight depressions over low ridges or ancient red rotting trunks showed where feet had trod. Twice she found a white unraveled thread on the hidden trail as if purposely dropped for her eyes to find.

It was several hours later when she smelled faint smoke. Cautioning Otter Boy not to speak, she kept on while the scent grew stronger, retracing her steps when it began to wane. Now she followed her nose into the south wind. She remembered the words, at the stream by the side of the mountain. At length she could see smoke standing in the forest, a clear blue showing it came from pine wood. In time she glimpsed the camp ahead among the butts of monster hemlocks on the bank of the creek at the foot of the steep mountain.

Then suddenly Nutiket, the sentinel, cried a warning, forms leaped from the ground, and she was dragged roughly into the middle of them.

"Ponchi! Let us alone," she ordered, shaking

them off. She told those who stood around her who she was.

They listened with unfriendly faces.

"You speak Indian. Your boy looks Indian. Why don't you know the Indian custom to send a messenger ahead to camp before blundering into it like a bear?"

"We are alone. Whom should I send?" she asked, keeping her eyes from the young Indian she had followed. "Should I send my young son as if I am a coward to come myself?"

She thought they might smile, as the most serious of Indians often did at a telling rejoinder in the village. But this was a war party and the faces stayed grim. They conferred with an elder. He had bitter eyes and deep wrinkles about his broad nose.

"What do you want here?" he wanted to know. "Maybe you are Schupijaw, the spy?"

"Does a spy come with a small son?" she asked. "I came to talk with you, my uncles."

"We do not have talk with women," he said coldly.

"In the Lenape town where I was raised, warriors came to talk to a woman. Her name was Amisheu. War parties came many miles to listen to her before they went into battle."

"I have heard of her," Big Nose said. "She was

an old woman, not a foolish young one. But speak.
We will listen and see if you are wise as she."

Stone Girl looked around her. The black eyes of
the painted men stared back at her. Beyond them,
tied to a young hemlock, she could see the pale
terrified face of a bedraggled Nan.

"Uncles, I see your young captive by the hemlock.
I know your good intentions toward her. You held
back the hatchet to make a daughter of her. You
want to wash off her cowardly white skin and put
on the brave skin of the Indian. You want to make
her as one of your own family. Uncles. When I was
young I was also taken captive by the Lenapes. My
cowardly white skin was washed away. I was made a
daughter of Feast Maker. He took out my pale
Yengwe heart and gave me the brave heart of the
Indian. I was shown how to plant and hoe corn,
to make meal, to cut up the deer and cook it and
dress and tan the skin. The great hunter and warrior Espan became my husband."

She paused.

"Uncles. I know this young captive by the hemlock. She is my young white sister. Uncles. You who
are fathers know that sisters are not always alike.
This sister you have taken is like the white deer that
does not inherit the strong brown coat of its fathers.

Uncles. I do not believe this girl will ever make a
brave Indian. She cries and complains. She speaks
spiteful things. She faints from long marches. She
makes bad faces over good food. I think she will
get the yellow vomit and die."

She waited in the customary Indian deliberation.

"Uncles. We do not like to see a sister die. I
come to make you a trade. The white trader cheats
you. I will not cheat you. I am Indian. I will make
you an honest trade. Give back the sickly complain-
ing white sister and I will go with you in her place.
You need not cut out my white heart or wash away
my white skin. They are already red like the Indian.
You need not teach or train me. Already I speak
the Indian tongue and know the Indian ways. Maybe
I am too old to be adopted as a daughter but I can
work as a wife and when my husband is old, my
son will keep us in game."

She looked around the circle when she finished
but could tell nothing from the daubed faces. Only
the eyes of the young Indian who had the curly
maple rifle looked thoughtfully at her. Now all with-
drew by the creek for council. It did not take long.
Returning, they stood in silence looking at her.
After a while the Indian with the broad nose and
bitter eyes spoke.

"Ochqueu, woman. We have heard you. You speak true enough about the small white sister. She insults us by crying at our companionship. She rejects us when we try to teach her the good life of the Indian. I think she will not breathe long. But that does not mean we are willing to see her go back. We will never return her to her white people."

He paused in the Indian fashion for his words to sink in and his eyes took on that strange delirious out-of-focus look she had seen in many warriors. He went on.

"Woman. You have lived too long among the Yengwes. An Indian would not ask such an unheard-of thing. Warriors do not make pacts with women. We are not children. If we let you take her home, how do we know you would keep your promise and return to us? You speak fine words. So does the little singing bird before he flies away and is never seen again. Woman. If we keep you here as hostage and send warriors with the child, the white man will kill them. His promise is like dead wood."

He picked up a dry stick, broke it between his fingers, and went on.

"Woman. Once the Indian listened to the white man. When the white man first came our fathers welcomed him. The white man said he wanted a little ground no bigger than a deer hide. He wanted to raise greens for his soup. The Indian gave him the ground. Then the white man put guns on it and made a fence around it so the Indian could not come in. The Indian was a child. He did not know the white man. He would not listen to the warnings of his prophets. Now the Indian knows. You see me standing here. I myself know the white man. As a boy the country around this place was my home. The land was Lenape land. My father's village stood near where the creek and river join. On the island in the river my father and his brothers raised corn and squash. All summer canoes would leap from the shore to the island and canoes from the island to our village on the land. At night our campfires burned on the island and the land. Our children played. Our old men dozed. The smoke from our village went straight up to the Great Spirit."

He halted again and the curious Indian ether leaped from his eyes.

"Young woman. Then the white man came. The Indian was driven off like cattle from his own land. He was pushed toward the setting sun. He took what he could with him, but he could not take the graves of his fathers. In the Pawpawing days some of us went back on pilgrimage looking for those graves. We could not find them. The white man had cut down the trees that waved over them. He had thrown away the rocks and logs laid against wolves and wolverines. He had plowed the bones to raise corn. Now you ask us to do favor to the white man who defiled our fathers' graves. You ask us to give his badly raised child back to him. Why should we do such a thing? It is better we should give him back the parings of his daughter's scalp. It is not wise to let such a white child grow up and bear children cowardly as she."

Stone Girl knew by the hostile faces there was no reprieve.

"Uncles. If the small sister must stay, maybe I can stay also. I think she will not cry so much with me and Otter Boy. My son can walk with her on the march and I can teach her the good ways of the Indian. Maybe then she can breathe longer."

The circle of black eyes gazed back at her. The mouth of the Indian with the broad nose turned down with disapproval.

"Young woman. It is better you do not come. But we are not like the white man. We will not drive our friends away. Gatati! Come. But if you try to take the child back, it will be bad for you and her, too."

Stone Girl's face was inscrutable. He went on.

"Young woman. I have more to say to you. You look Indian. You talk Indian. But the Yengwes have robbed you of the brave pitilessness of the Indian. It is not good to be sorry for the white deer. It is not good to be sorry for those who badly use you. Long ago the Great Spirit made a people. He called them the Guchuru. He gave them good country far south where flowers bloom in the wintertime. He gave them game, fish, corn, and squash. Another people came and saw the good Guchuru country. They went on the Guchuru land. They killed the Guchuru game and ate the Guchuru corn. The Guchuru did not fight or kill. Only felt sorry. They are hungry, the Guchuru said. Let them kill game, take corn and squash. Soon the Guchuru had nothing themselves to eat. Elkissa! said the Great Spirit. I have made Macho, something bad. What can I do with these people? They are good only to be sorry. Soon they starve. So he turned the Guchuru into a pigeon and called him Amemi. Now for a pigeon there was plenty food, nuts, seeds, berries. But the Amemi is still sorry. Every winter he goes south to visit the graves of his people. Summer and winter he still calls his name, Guchuru."

Stone Girl gazed back at him.

"It is a true story," she said. "My grandfather, Machilek, told it to me when I am a small girl. But I still wish to go with the small white sister."

"Bischi. Very well," he said. "Only remember that the Indian shoots the Guchuru."

Stone Girl met his eyes steadily until he turned away. Then she went to Nan, who threw herself upon her in a fit of tears and emotion. Stone Girl let her cry on her breast for a while but the hysterical child refused to stop. In the end she had to push her off, turn her back squarely, and walk away.

◆ *xiii* ◆

THE small white girl, Nan, lay on the ground shivering. How many days it had been since the savages carried her off, she didn't remember. Since the morning of horror at the preacher's house, her young mind had been a confusion of blood and scalps, painted faces, dark silence and harsh foreign tongues. It was a nightmare from which she couldn't awake. On the march she stumbled along as best she could. Nights she cried herself to sleep.

145

There were no days of the week here in the forest. All the child knew was her fixed hate for Claire, who called herself Stone Girl. At first when Claire had come to camp, Nan had turned to her eagerly as a familiar face from home, had thrown her small arms about her and poured out her misery. It was almost as if her own mother had returned from the grave. But Claire had turned out to be no better than the other Indians. She had ordered the child to stop crying, and when Nan cried the louder, she had done the unforgivable, and twisted the child's arm unbearably.

"Let me alone. You're as bad as the rest!" Nan had screamed, and slapped her.

If Claire minded, her face gave no indication. She looked almost pleased. From then on it was plain that she cared only to stir up the child's anger. When Nan shed tears or fell down on the march crying she wouldn't take another step, Claire would badger her till she jumped up and called Claire bad names that made the Indians laugh. They liked nothing better than a fight between these two. Their painted faces broke into grins at the child's fury. It looked as if Claire provoked her only to please the savages so she and Otter Boy could go free while she, Nan, had to be tied to a tree at night and by day hitched to Osgaak, the short Indian with the big head who claimed her.

Twice the party stayed two nights at the same place while the men left mysteriously by day. The first time the young savage with the curly maple rifle remained to guard camp. He and Claire spoke together in the Indian jargon.

"What do they talk so much about?" Nan asked Otter Boy.

"They talk about the Tuscarawas and Waldhoning and the Great Sweet Water," he told her.

When the savages returned that evening the girl shrank from the dripping scalps. Two days later the men left again and this time Osgaak stayed to guard camp. He was limping painfully now. On the last raid he had been wounded in the foot and now had it wrapped in a large clump of calico from some woman victim's dress. Claire warned Nan not to cross him or stir up his further hatred for the race that had lamed him. Once when Nan forgot herself and whined at him, he cuffed her to the ground, and when she cried out, he came for her with his scalp knife until Claire stopped him.

From that moment, the small girl sat frozen, afraid to move, and the savage turned his temper on Otter Boy. When Claire defended the boy, Osgaak shouted furiously at her and pointed for them to go, coming very close, pushing her back when she stood her ground. It enraged him to have Otter Boy push protectingly between them. He sent the boy sprawling and seized her.

Nan watched paralyzed. She saw Claire struggle with him and Otter Boy come to his mother's help, kicking and pounding the Indian's legs. The savage paid no attention till the boy's foot struck the lump of spotted calico. Then with a wild face he turned, seized him by the legs, and swung him in a rage against the nearest hemlock butt. There was no cry from the little fellow, no sound except a queer sickening almost liquid smack, and the small active body lay still.

When Nan looked at Claire she cried out despite herself. Claire had snatched the axe of some unknown white man from about the fire and thrown herself at the Indian. There was something in her face the child had never seen before. Osgaak went for his hatchet but before he could reach it, Claire's axe was on him. Then Nan covered her face with her hands and screamed.

She was still screaming pitifully when she opened them again. By this time Claire had picked up Otter Boy and was slowly rocking him in her arms, moan-

ing, saying unknown words over and over in the
Indian tongue, but there was no answer from the
boy. Never had Claire seemed more Indian than
now. Staring at her and the bloody scene, Nan felt
the great gulf between them. Hardly did Claire
seem to know the girl was there.

In the end when Claire turned, the leaden face
was as that of a stranger.

"They will kill when they find," she said, and held
out a hand to go.

"No!" Nan called out, holding back.

"You will burn for Osgaak," she told her.

"He has my chain that was Mamma's," the girl
cried, pointing to the bloody figure.

Claire unfastened the chain and cross from the
heavy wrist. The chain was finely woven. It seemed
like a thick gold cord in her hands. She hung it
slowly around Nan's neck. Then, with a deerskin
pouch of meal on her back, she was ready to go but
the child held back at the sight of Otter Boy in
Claire's arms. Surely she didn't expect to take that
frightening object with them.

"I don't want to!" she cried. Claire had to seize
a hand and drag her into the forest.

It seemed to the child that day that Claire must
be mad. She spoke little or nothing. She forced her

small companion into the rough woods instead of
easy paths, and refused to part with her dreadful
burden. At first the short bare legs of the corpse
swung limp as she tramped, but at the end they
stood out stiffly like the legs of a dead wolverine
Nan had once seen lying on its back near the inn.

They had not been gone long from camp when
they heard a hallooing behind them. Two shots followed, answered almost at once by others far distant.

"Somebody come back and find," Claire said.
"Now he call the rest."

All day till darkness closed in on them, Claire
insisted that they keep on. She stayed away from easy
paths, holding to the difficult side hills instead of
the valleys. Next day it was the same, treading on
rocks when possible, never on sticks, stepping over
water, never muddying a run, or leaving footprints
in wet places. Twice that day they heard musket
shots behind them. Morning and evening Claire
opened the pouch, quaffing the meal in her mouth
with her hand, washing it down with water, doing
the same to Nan, forcing down both meal and water
only to have the child vomit, after which Claire
chewed it herself first, mixed it a long time with her
own spit, forced the repulsive stuff into the child's
mouth and held the jaws shut till it was swallowed.

But the worst was the grisly object that went with them, the face a color it had never been in life, the eyes open, staring, seeing nothing, fixed in the terrifying mystery of death. At night Nan had to sleep with the dreadful thing close to her. Once she touched the lifeless face in her sleep and woke with the feel and smell of it on her hand. Then Claire had to choke her to stop the screaming.

The third day Nan said she could walk no more. It was barely daylight under the trees when Claire shook her awake. She had to twist her wrist to get her up and still her complaints. All day Claire harassed her, driving her on, refusing to let her speak aloud, treating her worse than the savages had. Surely, the child thought, there was no more danger, yet whenever they stopped for even a moment to rest, Claire sat poised for instant flight. By afternoon Nan could go no farther. She lay on the ground and refused to get up. Not even the fierce hallooing of voices from mountain to mountain roused her.

"I'd sooner stay and be killed," she whimpered, but Claire would have none of it, shaking the child, pinching her arms and legs, jerking her to her feet again and again, forcing her to take one step then another, and finally dragging her like a sack of deadwood over roots and rocks till Nan didn't know if she were alive or dead.

Late that afternoon Claire pulled her into a dense thicket of thorn trees. When the child complained at the formidable scratches, Claire clapped a hand over her mouth but not quickly enough. The dread hallooing sounded closer now. Soon low voices came from outside the thicket.

That night they lay there scarcely breathing. At the first sign of restlessness from Nan, the pitiless hand tightened on her small throat. When daylight came Claire made no movement to leave. Through the night all had been silence, and well into the morning, yet Claire sat there, rigid, head back, listening, sniffing. Hardly a muscle of her face changed when outside of the thicket sudden blood-curdling yells tried to flush them. A frightened bird flew out but Claire's only movement was to lay her hand in warning on Nan's mouth. The wild yells came again and someone shot into the thicket. Nan could hear the bullet plow through the leaves and into the ground nearby but Claire still sat motionless, her hand tight now on Nan's mouth so that the child could scarcely breathe. At last the guttural voices outside spoke freely together.

"They go now," Claire mouthed with her lips,

and in a little while the child heard the voices recede into the forest.

Still Claire would not leave. They spent a second night in the thicket before the hard journey was resumed. No musket shot was heard that day nor any voice but their own.

"Now we have time for the small valiant one," she said.

Next morning they came to a tiny run in a hollow. It bubbled from a sandy spring not far above. The water ran between low green banks deeply covered with moss. Great oaks and pines stood over them. On either side the slopes of the hollow sheltered the place. No sound reached them here but the soft sough of the wind high in the treetops and the tingle of the water over red shale rock into the tiny crystal pool beneath.

Claire stood looking around.

"It is the place," she said. "The Great Spirit has prepared it."

It was hard digging into the forest soil. The child watched incredulously as Claire worked on her knees with her hands. There was something inhuman about the scene, as if an animal burrowed with its paws. The only tools were Claire's fingers and flat rocks from the run to cut the roots. Her palms

scooped out the dark ground. The rest of the day
she worked at the small hole, deepening it, squaring
and leveling bottom and sides. It was late afternoon
when she finished. The hush that comes before sun-
down lay over everything when Nan saw Claire
rip strips from her own tattered skirt and wrap
them around the small form. Although the child
watched closely not a tear could she see in the gray
face. Repeating strange monotonous words over and
over in the Indian tongue, Claire pushed back the
black ground, patted the mound smooth with her
hands, then as twilight fell started to fetch pro-
tective rocks from the distant creek.

Suddenly Nan screamed. An Indian with his gun
stood at the edge of the hollow looking at them.
It was, the child recognized, the young savage with
the curly maple rifle who had been so thick with
Claire ever since she joined the war party. Claire
herself seemed unstartled to see him. The pair sat
down and talked in their strange tongue while Nan
fearfully watched and listened, understanding nothing. At the end the young savage took a hunk of
some hard black meat from his shirt, shaved thin
slices from it with his hunting knife, and gave the
dry tasteless shavings to the child, who spit them
out with loathing.

That night he stayed with them. Very early in the morning when it was still dark Nan awoke and found herself lying alone. Lifting her head, she saw the young savage gone and Claire sitting motionless beside the small grave. It was still night in the hollow, but as she watched, the first red rays of the sun came through and fell on two pine trunks on either side of the grave, lighting up the pillars and their grotesque roots with a reddish glow so that in the dimness they looked like the portal to some mysterious dark kingdom where only the wild and barbaric could obtain admission, where incomprehensible words were spoken and forest rites performed that no white child dare see or could understand if she did. Slowly the outlandish red light reached the fresh mound and it seemed as if this small grave between the two red columns was the threshold where all who entered had to pass.

◆ *xiv* ◆

THAT night deep in the forest Stone Girl thought she heard the faint distant bark of a dog. It could, she told herself, have been Gokhos, the long-eared owl. But yesterday she had glimpsed through the trees what looked like the Small Mountain she and Otter Boy had seen on the way out. Now it was early morning. The wind had turned to the east and before daylight very far away her ears caught the unmistakable crowing of roosters.

156

It was true then, she told herself, that her journey was almost over. A cruel feeling ran through her. Last time she had heard the Yengwe roosters Otter Boy had heard them with her. Now the bare ground around the stable would not know his small feet again. She would go to her room at night without him. The Great Spirit had given her Nan but had taken away the small valiant one.

It was like a white man's trade with the Indians, she thought bitterly. The son had been straight and sweet. The small sister was crooked and sour. Perhaps the Great Spirit realized the unfairness and had given her the mother's gold chain and cross to make up for it. Twice in anger Nan had thrown it away, once violently into Stone Girl's face and another time, knowing it would distress her, into a muddy run. Stone Girl had gone in after it, combing the stones and mud with her hands until she found it, and this time she had kept it. Around her neck it gave her a strange feeling. It was as if the lady with the yellow hair was telling her to keep it. This was her amulet. It would help her lift her head among the white people, give her favor with them. The lady with the yellow hair herself might even go with it, for she was her Guka, mamma, as well as Nan's, and when she, Stone Girl, was as small as

Nan, she was the white lady's Nitchan, or beloved
child.

She felt grateful for the amulet when she and
Nan came out of the forest. Before her lay the
barefaced Yengwe land cleared of the forest. When
she left, not a human but she and Otter Boy had
moved across it. That had been the Month When
the Deer Turns Red. Now it was the Month of
Roasting Ears. Daily since she left she had dropped
a small pebble into her deerskin pouch, a white one
while Otter Boy lived and a dark one since he went
into the ground. At the last count there had been
nearly forty pebbles, and now the white man was
back. From the forest came the high-handed sound
of Yengwe axes felling the trees and of arrogant
Yengwe shouts at horses dragging fresh logs for
rebuilding. Hardly had she stepped out of the forest
when a Yengwe guard sounded the alarm. Men with
guns rushed on them as at the sight of wolves. They
recognized neither her nor Nan, would scarcely believe when she told them who they were.

"We know Captain Stanton's daughter," one
said. "That's not her."

Stone Girl pushed on through them toward the
inn. It stood before her unchanged. Blue pine smoke
rose from its chimneys. As they drew close, Captain

Stanton himself came out of the front door. At the
sight of her father, the child gave a shrill cry. She
shook herself loose and started to run toward him.
When she came near she let herself fall to the ground
as if mortally wounded and crawled toward him
hysterically screaming.

"Nan! Is it you?" Captain Stanton cried in dis-
belief, gazing at the shrunken ragged figure. Then
he picked her up in his arms and carried her into
the inn.

Stone Girl stood for a while uncertain and alone.
She had not been asked in. The terrible look Captain Stanton gave her kept her back. She followed
to the porch steps and waited. From time to time
she felt others staring at her but they remained at
a distance. Not even Billy, the returned hostler,
came near or spoke to her. Didn't they know who
she was, she wondered, with her skirt whipped into
pieces and cut off nearly to her thighs, with her
legs, arms, and shoulders black with travel and torn
by brush and thorns, her flesh, like Nan's, almost to
the bone? She heard the time measurer in the inn
call twice before Captain Stanton came out.

"We don't know if she will live or not," he said
grimly.

"Otter Boy die but Nan live," Stone Girl told

him. "Just give little to eat. Only thin boiled meat
the first day."

"I think we know best how to take care of her,"
Captain Stanton told her caustically. "What we
don't know is what to do with you."

"I be all right," Stone Girl assured him.

"Maybe you will," he agreed bitterly. "You can
thank your heathen gods we are white and Christian
and are not inclined to take revenge on you for your
aid and comfort to the enemy."

"I am not enemy," she told him.

He looked at her with hard eyes.

"There's no use lying, Claire. We know all. Your
savage friends brutally murdered and scalped the
people who stayed here, including my own mother.
But the savages never harmed you. Nan says you
joined them the first day. You went along willingly
and carried and cooked for them on their murderous
way. Only after a long time when your boy died
did you leave them. Even then, Nan says, one of
the savages followed and stayed with you. Perhaps
this same Indian is in cahoots with you now and you
expect to get something out of bringing her back."

"I don't expect something," she told him. "She
is my sister."

His lower lip drew down.

"You must know, Claire, that she is not your
sister and never has been. If she had been, you might
not have abused her the way you did. You must also
know that Nan has told us everything. Not that she
had to. We could see the marks ourselves where you
twisted and pinched her and at night where you
choked her. The marvel is that she's still alive. Her
whole body is a mass of bruises, not to speak of
hundreds of cuts and scratches. We took festered
thorns from her legs and feet. She told us you
dragged her through the worst terrain you could
find, over rocks and logs, through bushes and thorn
thickets. When she couldn't walk any more, you beat
her till she'd manage to go on."

"She must come home," Stone Girl said. "Can't
die in woods. I go through bushes and thickets, too."

"You're a grown woman, or almost. Nan's a child.
Why didn't you carry her?"

"I carry sometimes," Stone Girl told him. "Indian don't carry all the time. Indian child must walk
to be strong."

"Well, you needn't have practiced your Indian
cruelty on my child," he said harshly. "And you
needn't have practiced the Indian art of stealing.
Not after I took you into my employ and trusted
you."

"Indian don't steal," she told him. "Only take back what white man takes from Indian."

"Well, there's the painting of my wife," he reminded her. "You surely don't believe I or anybody else took that from the savages? One of my men found it where you abandoned it in the woods. You must have found it too heavy and cumbersome to take along."

"I take it out of the house," Stone Girl testified. "If house burns, the lady with yellow hair don't burn."

His mouth grew sarcastic.

"What else did you 'take' from us, as you call it?" And when she did not reply, "How about my wife's gold chain and cross that belonged to Nan? I think I see it on you now. If you'll return it to me, I'll give it back to its rightful owner."

Stone Girl stood very still. Presently she unclasped the chain and with eyes fastened on the cherished object gave it to him.

"Now you can go to your room until I decide what to do with you," he told her. "I think you had better stay there for a while. One of my men who lost his wife or child to your friends might take a potshot at you. Meantime you better be sorry."

"White father—" she began.

"I am not your father," he interrupted sharply.

"Your black book says we are all related from Adam," she reminded. "The Indian believed this long before. He calls every man father, grandfather, brother, cousin, or uncle."

Captain Stanton did not reply. She went on.

"White father. You say to be sorry. Your black book says you white people killed your god. Hang him on tree. Now you white people sorry. Your preacher says Indian must be sorry, too. Why must Indian be sorry? He didn't kill white god. It was white man's doing. White father. This happened a long time ago. Now white man be sorry. Maybe after long time white man be sorry he rob Indian. But where is Indian then? White father. Maybe someday white father be sorry he rob daughter. But where is daughter then?"

"I don't follow you," Captain Stanton said. "I am extremely sorry for my youngest daughter. My other daughter is in Philadelphia. You are a stranger to us. You say you are Indian. Your boy certainly was Indian. You yourself act like one, you think like one, you talk like one, you sympathize with the savages, and you come back half naked like one. I want you to stay out of sight in your room. When it's safe to come down and work out your con-

tract, I'll try to send you up some clothes so you
don't look indecent."

Stone Girl turned and made her way toward the
stable. At the watering trough she stopped to wash
herself as best she could, using her teeth to pull the
thorns and sand to reveal thighs and upper parts
white under the caked blackness of travel. Her move-
ments were deliberate and with dignity. She knew
eyes were watching. If some white man wanted to
shoot, she told herself, here she was.

Up in the stable she stood a long time at the door
to the stifling room. It was hard to go in. Everything here spoke of Otter Boy. She remembered now
the dream she had had in this place of Tiquensukey,
the black panther cub. She had played with it in her
dream and the claws of Tiquensukey had torn her
flesh. She had not understood the dream then. It was
not her flesh but her heart, she told herself now, that
had been torn. Oh, she knew that the warrior who
died in battle went into the next world with merit
that set him above those who died in their beds. But
Otter Boy was so little. He was not yet old enough
to hunt. How would he live in the next world? If
Espan or her father or grandfather saw him, they
would teach him. But how could he find them among
so many who had gone before?

She was still there when Billy called shortly from
the stable below.

"There's a plate down here for you."

She made no immediate move to go. They had set
scraps out to her as to a dog. She would wait, she
told herself, till she felt like a dog or had a dog's
hunger. Then the image of Otter Boy rose in her
mind and reproved her. For weeks, she remembered,
she had fetched his rations out to him on a plate
from the kitchen and never once had he refused or
reproached her. Quietly she went down and ate sitting on the thick dust of the stable stairs. Afterward she washed the plate at the watering trough
and left plate and spoon by the back door of the inn.

Nights that followed she lay awake and listened.
Below her the horses moved restlessly in their stalls.
From outside came the call of Gokhos, the hoot owl,
now near over bare Yengwe fields, now far away
over forest and river. His distant voice resembled
that of the dog, but no dog ever spoke in such measured tones. She missed the warm little ball of Otter
Boy curled up beside her. The days were almost as
hard to bear, shut up in this place with everyone else
free to go and the sound of their superior voices
reaching her.

The moon was in the half round when the sum-

mons came. It was Gokhos again, but this time the
call rode one of the four winds, ever in the same
place. She rose and went quietly down the stable
steps thick with the seed of the hay. She had started
toward the dark rim of the forest when the lighted
windows of the inn drew her. She crept closer for a
last look. Her feet made scarcely a sound on the
veranda. At the window of the room with the gold
chair of curved legs she stopped. Captain Stanton
had come home late. She had heard his horse brought
into the stable. Now through the glass she saw him
and Nan sitting together intimately at a small table
where a new girl served them supper. A fire burned in
the fireplace. Candles flickered on the white cloth, on
table silver, on brass about the warm room, and
on the painting of the lady with yellow hair that hung
on the wall. The lady's face seemed almost alive tonight, the eyes sad, peering at Stone Girl through
the pane. It was as if they tried to tell her something
but the thoughts of white people were hard to understand. Those eyes, she felt, would always haunt her
and never would she know what they tried to say.

At last she turned from the inn. The cool sympathetic hands of her aunt, the Night, received her.
Her brother, the West Wind, blew softly upon her
with his sweet forest breath. Her very old uncle, the
Moon, looked down upon her with compassion. At

the edge of the forest a figure detached itself from a tree and stood beside her.

"It is ready?" the familiar voice asked in Delaware.

"I have the blanket," she answered.

"It is a long journey," he reminded.

"I have come. I can go," she said.

"On the Allegheny Sipu we will find a boat," he promised. "It will take us to the small river of Quipias, the buffalo. Quipias will bear us to the lake, and a stream I do not know the name of will take us to the Great Sweet Water. There is a fort and two portages if you can carry."

"I can carry," Stone Girl said.

"Elke, good. First we camp where the small warrior breathes no more. You can visit the grave and make what you need for yourself till you are strong. I will fill your bowels with game. Then we will run up the mountains. I climbed them with my cousin. I know the way."

She turned. Behind her the inn rose above the bare fields. Its yellow eyes looked after her like the eyes of the lady on the wall but the whitewashed stables behind were a ghost in the night.

She turned back to True Son, who had stood waiting with Indian patience. He, too, he told her, had once taken leave of his father's house at night.

Now with Stone Girl behind him, he struck out along the edge of the dark woods, heading toward the ancient path that led to the mountains behind which the sun set.

As she marched, the words of another journeyer came back to her. It had been the one they called Milhilusis, old man, who had asked for refuge in their village when she had become a wife. See Fire, who had given him room in his cabin, said he was of the Cannois tribe that some call the Canawese or Kanhawas, but Espan declared he was of the far-away Mahicanni or Stone Axe people whom some called the Schainkooks or River Indians who had lost their lands again and now must move once more. No one knew how old he was, but he told See Fire that the day he did not walk out he would die. After-noons, sun, rain, or snow, he wandered about the vil-lage chanting his lament. At first it was hard to understand him but gradually the village learned his words by heart. Stone Girl had never been able to forget them. The lines came back to her now to the rhythm of her step as she tramped.

I am the wanderer. I am the exile,
Banished to live in a country of strangers,
Scanning their faces. None are familiar.

Where are my fathers? Where are my people?
They are no more. Their lands have been taken,
Their graves are defiled, by barbarians rifled.
Often at daybreak, often at twilight,
Often in dreams rise the bitter longings
For faces of brothers, for songs of their triumph,
For sight of their village with blue smoke curling.
Rises no more the sun on their lodges.
Rises no moon to the sound of the love lute,
The heart is a shell, the limbs are the turtle,
The blood crawls slow like brown swamp water.
Only the heart like the wind never ceases,
Calling old names, the names of companions.
There is no answer. Sorrow walks with me.
Grief goes before me. No one comes after.
I am the exile. I am the wanderer,
Destined to die in a country of strangers.

A NOTE ABOUT THE AUTHOR

CONRAD RICHTER was born in Pennsylvania, the son, grandson, nephew, and great-nephew of clergymen. He was intended for the ministry, but at thirteen he declined a scholarship and left preparatory school for high school, from which he was graduated at fifteen. After graduation he went to work. His family on his mother's side was identified with the early American scene, and from boyhood on he was saturated with tales and the color of Eastern pioneer days. In 1928 he and his small family moved to New Mexico, where his heart and mind were soon captured by the Southwest. From this time on he devoted himself to fiction. *The Sea of Grass* and *The Trees* were awarded the gold medal of the Societies of Libraries of New York University in 1942. *The Town* received the Pulitzer Prize in 1951, and *The Waters of Kronos* won the 1960 National Book Award for fiction. His other novels include *The Fields* (1946), *The Light in the Forest* (1953), *The Lady* (1957), *A Simple Honorable Man* (1962), *The Grandfathers* (1964), and *The Aristocrat*, published just before his death in 1968.

This book is composed in Linotype "Scotch". This style of type came into fashion in England and the United States by way of fonts cast at the foundry of Alex. Wilson & Son at Glasgow in 1833. It was a style of letter that echoed the "classical" taste of the time, and would seem to have been inspired by the kind of letter-shapes that result when you cut lettering on a copper plate with a graver—just as visiting-cards are cut now. It is more precise and *vertical* in character than the "old style" types (such as Caslon) that it displaced.

The typography and binding are based on designs by W. A. Dwiggins. The book was composed, printed, and bound by The Haddon Craftsmen, Inc., Scranton, Pennsylvania.